Enid B

The Fly-Away Cottage

...and other stories

Bounty
BOOKS

Published in 2015 by Bounty Books,
a division of Octopus Publishing Group Ltd,
Carmelite House
50 Victoria Embankment,
London EC4Y 0DZ
www.octopusbooks.co.uk

An Hachette UK Company
www.hachette.co.uk
Enid Blyton ® Text copyright © 2015 Hodder & Stoughton Ltd.
Illustrations copyright © 2015 Octopus Publishing Group Ltd.
Layout copyright © 2015 Octopus Publishing Group Ltd.

Illustrated by Maureen Bradley.

ISBN: 978-0-75372-947-2

A CIP catalogue record for this book is available from the
British Library.

Printed and bound in the United Kingdom

3 5 7 9 10 8 6 4

CONTENTS

The Fly-Away Cottage

Joanna and Paul looked out of the nursery window. It was pouring with rain, and they had to go across the fields to fetch the eggs from the farm.

"What a nuisance!" said Paul. "It's such a long way down the road and over the hill to the farm when it's raining."

"Well, let's take the short cut through the woods," said Joanna. "We can put on our big rubber boots and our macs and sou'westers, and we shall be sheltered from the wind if we walk through the wood. It won't take us very long."

So they put on their rubber boots, and their mackintoshes and oilskin hats. They took the basket for the eggs, called goodbye to their mother and set out. It *was* raining hard! There were big puddles everywhere, and the rain splashed into them and made them bigger still! The wind blew hard too, and altogether it was a very stormy, windy day.

Soon the two children came to the woods. They were glad to get among trees, for they were more sheltered then. They walked through the dripping trees, over the soaking grass. Then suddenly came such a gale blustering through the woods that the children were quite frightened.

"I hope the wind won't blow any trees down on us," said Joanna, looking round at the trees bent almost double in the gale. "I wish there was somewhere for us to shelter in just until this storm is over, Paul. Is there any cottage near that we could go to?"

"No," said Paul. "I've never seen any cottage here at all."

Just as he spoke, Joanna cried out in surprise and pointed to the left.

"Look, Paul! There's the funniest cottage I've ever seen. What are those

things growing out of each side of it?"

It certainly was a strange cottage. Jutting out at each side of it were big feathery wings. They were perfectly still, and drooped a little in the rain. The cottage was very small, and had a yellow front door with one chimney that twisted here and there in the wind.

"It's the funniest cottage I've ever seen," said Paul. "I don't know whether to go to it or not. It looks odd to me. Goodness knows who might live there – a witch perhaps, or an enchanter. It's just the sort of cottage you see in a book."

The two children stood looking at it, and the rain fell more and more heavily on them.

"It's raining cats and dogs," said Paul, and, my goodness me, just as he said that, his words came true. It really *did* begin to rain cats and dogs! A large black kitten fell on Joanna's head, and a little white dog fell down by Paul. Then two tabby cats tumbled near Joanna and three collies around Paul. The children stood looking at them in amazement. Then they looked up at the sky. It was full of cats and dogs, all falling to earth like rain!

"Quick! Run to the cottage!" said Paul, in a fright. "We don't want hundreds of dogs and cats on our heads! It must be a very bad storm if it rains cats and dogs!"

The Fly-Away Cottage

So they ran through the falling cats and dogs to the funny little cottage. Joanna thought she saw its wings move a little as they came near. A black cat fell on to her shoulder and made her squeal. She rushed to the cottage door and turned the handle. She and Paul ran inside and slammed the door behind them.

A smell of newly-made cakes was in the cottage. The children gazed around the room they were in. A small woman with green wings growing out of her shoulders looked round at them from the fireplace.

"Now then, now then, what do you mean by rushing in like that without so much as a knock at the door or a ring?"

she said grumpily. "Here I've got my oven door open and my cakes are baking as well, and you come in and make a draught like that. It's enough to make them all go flat, so it is."

The children were so surprised to see such a funny person that they couldn't speak. The little woman was fat and round and she wore a sort of sun-bonnet on her head. Her cheeks were hot from the fire, and she shut her oven door with a slam.

"Well?" she said. "Haven't you a tongue in your heads, either of you? What do you want? Have you come to buy any of my cakes?"

"No," said Paul. "We didn't know you sold them. Are you a fairy?"

"I'm a pixie woman," said the funny little person, taking off her spectacles and polishing them on her big white apron. "I'm the famous Mother Mickle-Muckle, whose cakes are bought for all the best parties in Fairyland and Witchland. Haven't you ever heard of me?"

"No," said Joanna, feeling rather excited to see a real pixie person. "I'm so sorry if our opening the door has spoilt your cakes. But, you see, it's raining cats and dogs outside and we had to run for shelter."

"Cats and dogs!" said the pixie woman in surprise. "Nonsense!"

Just as she spoke a large brown and white dog fell down the chimney into the fire. It jumped out at once and ran barking round the kitchen. Mother Mickle-Muckle picked up a frying-pan and ran after it.

"Get out, you clumsy creature!" she said. "I won't have animals in my nice clean kitchen!"

She opened the door and the dog ran out into the wood. But no sooner had the pixie woman shut it than two big cats fell down her chimney, and when they had jumped out on the hearthrug they began to fight, spitting and snarling at one another in a spiteful manner. The pixie picked up a rolling-pin and rushed angrily at the cats.

They flew at her and scratched her on the hand. Then out of the window they jumped, still hissing at one another.

"Look at that now!" said Mother Mickle-Muckle, showing her hand to the children. "I won't stay here a minute longer! I hate dogs and cats falling down my chimney! Cottage, fly to Topsy-Turvy Land!"

Before the children could say a word the cottage spread its two feathery wings and flew up into the air! Yes, it

really did! Joanna rushed to a window and she saw its wings beating the air like a bird's, and, as she watched, the trees were left behind and the cottage rose high into the air.

"Ooh!" cried Joanna in the greatest astonishment. "The cottage is flying away!"

"Of course," said the pixie, busy rolling out some pastry on the kitchen table. "It's Fly-Away Cottage, didn't you know that? It's famous all over the world."

"Well, *I've* never heard of it," said Joanna. "Have you, Paul?"

"Never," said Paul, looking in wonder out of the window, gazing at fields and woods below them.

"Then you are two silly, ignorant children," said Mother Mickle-Muckle quite crossly. "I don't know where you go to school, if they don't teach you things like that."

"I wish we *were* taught things like that!" said Joanna. "It would be much more exciting to learn about this Fly-Away Cottage, and you, than about bays and rivers."

Mother Mickle-Muckle was pleased. She took a plate of chocolate buns from the cupboard and put them down in front of the children.

"You can each have two," she said. "We shan't arrive at Topsy-Turvy Land for another hour or two. Take off your coats and hats and sit down."

"Whatever will Mother say if we don't go back to dinner?" said Paul. "I don't think we ought to go to Topsy-Turvy

land, Mother Mickle-Muckle, though I'd love to."

"You'll *have* to go," said the pixie, popping another tin of cakes into the oven. "I am taking some cakes to the Big Little Goblin for his party this afternoon and he would turn me into a biscuit or an ice-cream if I were late."

"Big Little Goblin!" said Joanna in surprise. "Nobody can be big and little, too."

"Oh, can't they?" said Mother Mickle-Muckle, rolling out some more dough. "Well, let me tell you, my clever little girl, that the Big Little Goblin is little in height but very big in width. That is, he is very short and very fat, and he is the King of Topsy-Turvy Land because he is the stupidest person there."

"Then why do they make him King?" asked Paul, astonished.

"Oh, everything is upside-down in Topsy-Turvy Land," said the pixie. "The stupidest is King and the cleverest is a beggar. Now just sit down and keep quiet whilst I decorate these cakes.

We'll be passing over the sea in a little while, and you can watch the ships."

It was strange to be in a little cottage flying high above the clouds. The two children looked out of the windows and saw the ships on the sea, and then at last they were over land again. The cottage swooped down and landed with a bump on a little hill. The children were thrown off their feet, but Mother Mickle-Muckle didn't seem to mind.

She put some cakes into a basket and opened the door. "Come along," she said.

The children followed her – and how surprised they were to see the land they had come to. Everything was Topsy-Turvy!

The houses stood on their chimneys, and the people had to have ladders to get up to their front doors. It was really most peculiar. The people walked the right way up but they all wore a large boot or shoe on their heads instead of a hat. Joanna and Paul wanted to laugh whenever they met anyone.

The people were mostly small and

fat, and they all had funny little button noses and pointed ears. They wore their coats back to front and they talked very loudly in high voices.

The Big Little Goblin lived in a small cottage and didn't look a bit like a king. He wore a red button-boot on his head, and round one of his legs was a golden crown. He took the basket of cakes from Mother Mickle-Muckle and peered at them to see if they were all right.

"He's a funny sort of king," said Joanna, when they came out of the cottage. "I should have thought he would have lived in that big palace over there." She pointed to a high, shining palace a little way off.

"Oh, that's where the cleverest man lives, the beggar I told you of," said the pixie woman. "This is Topsy-Turvy Land, remember. Beggars live in palaces and kings live in cottages."

Joanna stopped to watch a Topsy-Turvy Man walk up the ladder to his upside-down front door. She thought it must be very funny to walk on ceilings and see your fire burning upside-down.

"Come along, come along," said Mother Mickle-Muckle impatiently. "I must get to Giant Too-Tall's before one o'clock with a jam roll."

They hurried back to where the Fly-Away Cottage was waiting for them. It was waving its feathery wings in the air, and was so anxious to be away that it rose up in the air almost before Joanna had gone through the door. She nearly fell out as it rose with a jerk and Paul just caught her in time and pulled her into the kitchen.

"We'd better have our dinner whilst the cottage is flying to Giant Too-Tall's," said the pixie woman, and she set the

table with a white cloth. For their dinner she gave them hot ginger buns, cherry pie and cheese biscuits straight from the oven. They liked it very much. The cottage flew steadily through the air whilst they ate, and when next the children looked out of the window they saw a big black cloud in front of them with something glittering in the middle of it.

"There's a castle right in the middle of the cloud!" said Joanna in surprise. "Goodness, how wonderful!"

Sure enough, there was! The cottage flew into the thick cloud and set itself down in the castle yard. The pixie woman took a small jam roll out of the oven.

"Is that for a giant?" asked Paul, laughing. "Goodness, he must be a small giant!"

"You wait and see!" said Mother Mickle-Muckle, and she opened the door of her cottage.

"Coo-ee!" she called, in a high, bird-like voice. "Coo-ee!"

The door of the great castle opened and out came an enormously tall giant with eyes as big as dinner-plates. Joanna and Paul felt quite frightened and ran back into the cottage.

"Have you brought my jam roll?" called a thundering voice and the cottage shook from top to bottom.

"Yes, come and get it," answered the pixie woman and she held out the jam roll she had made. The children saw a big hand come down to get it and dear me, what a very peculiar thing happened! As soon as the jam roll touched the giant's hand, it grew ten times as large, and was the biggest jam roll the children had ever seen in their lives!

"Thanks," said the giant's booming voice, and he gave the pixie woman a coin as large as a saucer. But as soon as it touched her hand it became small, and she slipped it in her pocket.

"Have you got visitors in your Fly-Away Cottage?" suddenly asked the giant and he bent down and looked through one of the windows. "Ho, children! Come along with me and play with my daughter!"

"Good gracious me, no!" cried the pixie woman. "She would think they were dolls and would break them in a second."

"You give them to *me*!" said the giant and he tried to open the window to get at the children. But the pixie woman slapped his hand smartly with her rolling-pin so that he cried out in pain, and she called out: "Fly away, cottage, to the cave of the dwarf!"

The cottage at once spread its wings and left the black cloud with its great castle towering in the midst. It flew into the blue sky, and the two children were

delighted to leave the tall giant behind.

The cottage flew lazily along, and the pixie woman looked at the clock. It said three o'clock. She tapped sharply on the wall of the cottage and cried: "Now then, Fly-Away Cottage, hurry up or we shan't be at the dwarf's cave in time for tea. He must have his cherry buns for it's his birthday party."

The cottage began to flap its wings so fast that it jerked about and the children sat down suddenly on the floor. Cups flew off the dresser and a chair fell on to the pixie woman's toe so that she cried out in pain.

"Now, now," she shouted, banging the cottage wall with her rolling-pin, "what are you thinking of, cottage, to fly so fast? Be sensible. We don't want to be jerked out of the windows." They were passing over the sea again, but it was a very odd sea, for it was bright yellow, streaked with pink.

Time went on and soon the hands of the clock pointed to four. A mountain came in sight, standing right up in the middle of the yellow sea, just like a pointed island. The cottage flew to

it and perched on the very top. The children wondered if it would slide down – and no sooner did they wonder it than the cottage *did* slide down! What a funny feeling it was – just like going down in a very swift lift!

Bump! The cottage reached the bottom and the children fell over again. When they picked themselves up they saw the pixie woman going out of the door with a basket of cherry buns.

"Don't come with me," she said. "The Tick-Tock Dwarf is bad-tempered and might want to keep you for servants. Stay here."

So the children stayed where they were, and peeped out of the door. Joanna saw a strange-looking flower growing not far off and ran out to get it. As she stooped to pick it she heard a voice say: "Ha! Here are some children! Let's take them prisoners!"

She looked up and saw a tiny dwarf staring at her, and not far away were about a dozen others like him. They all had long beards reaching to the ground, and wore long-pointed shoes on their big feet. Joanna was frightened and she ran back to the cottage and slammed the door, hoping that the pixie woman would return very soon.

But she didn't come. The dwarfs surrounded the cottage and came closer and closer. Paul locked the door and fastened all the windows.

"I believe there's a dwarf coming down the chimney!" he said suddenly, and sure enough, there was!

"They'll capture us!" said Joanna, looking ready to cry. Paul peeped out of the window to see if the pixie woman was coming but there was no sign of her.

So in despair he cried out to the cottage: "Fly-Away Cottage, please fly away from here and take us home!"

At once, the cottage spread its wings and rose into the air! The children were so glad. The dwarf who was climbing down the chimney got out again in a great hurry and jumped to the ground just in time. The cottage flew over the

yellow and pink sea at a great pace. Joanna and Paul were glad to leave the dwarfs' island but they were worried about the pixie woman. What would she do? Would she have to live on the island all her life?

Suddenly they heard a cross voice shouting. They looked out of the

window. Behind them flew the pixie woman trying her hardest to keep up with the cottage.

"Open the door and let me in!" she shouted. "You stupid, silly children, open the door."

They opened the door, and Mother Mickle-Muckle flew in. She sat down by the fire and panted. She was very cross with them.

"Flying off with my cottage like that!" she said. "I never heard of such a thing!

I shall take you both straight back home. I really don't know what you'll do next!"

The children were *so* glad to be flying home. They had had quite enough adventures for one day. Just as the clock hands pointed to twenty past four the cottage flew downwards, and the children saw that they were in their very own garden! How glad they were! It had stopped raining, and the sun was shining. They took up their mackintoshes and hats and stepped out of the strange Fly-Away Cottage.

"Good-bye, Mother Mickle-Muckle," they said. "Thank you for our nice dinner and all the adventures."

"You're welcome to them," said the little pixie woman, putting another tin of cakes into her oven and slamming the door. "Come and see me again when it's raining cats and dogs!"

Off they ran and the last they saw of the Fly-Away Cottage was a speck in the air that looked like a kite as the cottage flapped away to the west where the sun was sinking slowly. "I *do* hope we see it again if ever it rains cats and dogs," said Joanna. I'd like to, too, wouldn't you?

Lazy Lenny

Lenny was lucky. He was down by the sea for a holiday, with his three cousins, Karen, Rachel and George. They were having great fun. They all had fishing-nets, spades, pails and balls, so there was plenty for them to do.

The only thing was – Lenny was so lazy. He would only dig for a few minutes in the sand, and then stop. He would only fetch water two or three times in his pail and then he wanted to lie down in the sun. The others thought he was very tiresome.

"He leaves us to finish everything," said Karen. "He's lazy."

"It would do him good to dig hard every day," said George. "He's too fat."

"He just digs a few spadefuls and then leaves us to do all the hard work," said

Rachel. "And when we have finished our castle, or our moat, he expects to be allowed to sit on the top, or paddle in the moat. It's not fair."

"I vote we *make* him work hard today," said Karen. "We will dig a simply enormous castle, and we will make him help. We just won't let him say no!"

So when they were down on the beach that day Karen spoke to Lenny.

"Lenny, we're going to build the most enormous castle we have ever built before. You're to help us."

"It's too hot to dig," said Lenny, lazily.

"We're not going to listen to excuses like that," said George, crossly. "You've got to do your bit. Come on, now – get up and help."

Lazy Lenny

"I've left my spade at home," said Lenny, lying back on the sand.

"We'll soon put that right," said Karen, and she ran up the beach, across the road, and into the house where they were all staying. She soon came back with Lenny's spade. "There you are, Lazy!" she said, throwing it down beside him. "Now come and dig."

"My spade is so bent, it's no use," said Lenny. He really was marvellous at making excuses.

The other children looked at the spade. It was an iron one, and certainly it had got rather bent.

"Well, George has two spades. He will lend you one of his," said Rachel, impatiently. "George, throw it across."

George threw his second spade across to Lenny. It hit him on the ankle.

"Oooh, oooh!" said Lenny, pretending to be hurt, and rubbing his ankle. "Now I shan't be able to stand!"

"Don't be a baby," said Karen. "Get up and dig."

"I'm not going to use that silly baby

wooden spade," said Lenny. "It's too small for me."

"Well, what are you going to do then?" asked Karen. "Aren't you ever going to dig again?" You say you can't use your spade because it's bent, and you won't use George's because it's a wooden one. What are you going to do?"

"My mother gave me some money this morning to buy a new spade," said Lenny, and he took a pound out of his pocket to show the others. "I shall get one at that nice shop on the corner, that has hundreds of spades hanging outside."

"Well, go and buy it now, then, and you can help us to dig," said George. "Go on. Get up and buy it. You are always making excuses."

"I just want to see these aeroplanes flying over," said Lenny, and he lay on his back to watch them. The others began their digging. Lenny watched the planes and played with his money. The planes flew right over and disappeared.

"Go on, Lenny, and buy your

spade now," said Karen. "The planes have gone."

"I want to watch that dog having a bathe," said Lenny. "Don't bother me. I'll go in a minute."

The dog splashed in and out of the water, barking. Then he ran to his master. The three children looked at Lenny. He knew he would have to go now. He could think of no more excuses.

So up he got and brushed the sand from his shorts. Then he felt in his pocket for the pound he had been playing with.

It wasn't there! He felt again and again, but no, the pound was gone. It must have fallen into the sand. He bent down to look for it.

"What's the matter now?" asked George.

"I've lost my pound," said Lenny. "Come and help me to look for it."

"No," said George. "You can see we are busy. You wouldn't come and help us when we asked you to. I don't see why we should stop digging our castle to dig for your pound. You find it yourself!"

Well, poor Lenny hunted the whole of the morning for that pound, and he couldn't find it! It was most extraordinary. He took George's little wooden spade and dug up the sand all round him, working so hard that

he panted like a dog. But he couldn't find anything.

"Look at Lenny! He's working far harder than we wanted him to!" laughed Karen. She couldn't help feeling a bit sorry for Lenny, because she knew how horrid it is to lose anything. But she felt that it was very good for him to have to work so hard to find it.

Dinnertime came and still the money was not found. Lenny went home in tears and told his mother. She was cross.

"I shall not give you another

pound," she said. "Why didn't you stop at the shop on your way down to the beach and buy a new spade at once, as I told you to? I knew you would lose it if you took it down on the sand."

"I haven't a spade to dig with," wept Lenny. "Mine's bent."

"Well, I'll give you my wooden one," said George. "You didn't want it this morning, but now that you can't get a new one, perhaps you would like it."

"And you can use my spade when I'm not digging if you like," said Karen, kindly.

"And mine too," said Rachel, slipping her hand into Lenny's. He felt comforted.

"You're kind," he said. "I wouldn't help you this morning, but all the same

you want to help *me*. I won't be lazy
again. I'll help you to dig this afternoon,
and I'll dig like anything. You just see!
You haven't quite finished the castle, so
there's still some to be done."

"Good boy!" said Karen. "That's the
way to talk. We'll think a lot of you if
you behave like that."

Lenny ate his dinner and thought
quite a lot while he ate it. He knew he
was lazy. He knew that he left most of
the hard work to his cousins. Now he
had lost his pound because he had been
too lazy to dig, too lazy to go and get
his new spade, too lazy to do anything

but lie in the sand and watch the others at work.

"But now I'm going to behave properly," he decided. "I'll show the others what I can really do. I'm sure I dug harder in the sand, looking for my pound this morning, than they dug when they were building their castle!"

So that afternoon, when they went down on the beach, it was a very different Lenny who set to work on the castle. The others were nice to him.

"That spade of George's really is too small for you," said Karen. "I'll lend you mine and use the wooden one instead. I don't mind."

"No – he can have my big spade," said George, generously. "Here you are Lenny."

"I'll go and fetch water for the moat round the castle, and Lenny can use my spade," said Rachel.

Lenny looked at her. "But you don't like fetching water. You like digging," he said.

"Oh, well, that doesn't matter," said

Rachel, and she picked up her pail. She pushed her spade into Lenny's hand and he began to dig.

He dug two or three times, lifting up big loads to put on top of the high castle – and then, as he lifted up the third spadeful, something fell from the sand into the moat round the castle – something round.

"Oh – my POUND!" yelled Lenny, in the greatest surprise and delight. "Look – my pound!"

He picked it up. The others crowded round him, just as pleased as he was. "Now you'll be able to buy yourself a new spade after all!" said Karen. "Oh, I *am* glad you've found it."

"I'm going off to the shop straight away," said Lenny, and he sped off up the beach and on to the front. He went to the shop that sold spades – but he didn't buy a spade. No – he bought a tiny red and blue boat for Karen that cost forty pence. He bought a floating fish for Rachel that cost fifteen pence. And he bought a little grey battleship for George that cost forty-five pence. That made up the pound.

He rushed back to the beach. "George! Karen!, Rachel! Look what I've got for you!"

The children looked and were thrilled. "Oh, what lovely little things," said Karen. "But didn't you buy yourself a spade then, Lenny?"

"No," said Lenny. "I'll use George's old one, if he'll let me. There wasn't anything wrong with it really. All that was wrong was my own laziness! These little presents for you are my way of saying I'm sorry. Come on – let's finish the castle."

Well, wasn't that fine of Lenny! The other children thought the world of him after that, and when they told their own mother what Lenny had bought with his pound, what do you think she did? Yes – she went off and bought a new spade for Lenny – so everyone was as pleased as could be!

Dicky Dawdle's Adventures

Dicky Dawdle was just like his name. He was a real dawdler! He dawdled over his dressing in the morning, so that he was always late for breakfast. He was slow over his porridge, so that he was always late for school. He dreamed over his lessons, so he nearly always missed his playtime!

One day he met a little pixie fellow ambling down the lane, his hands in his pockets and his coat wrongly buttoned up.

"Hello," said Dicky in surprise, for he saw that the little fellow was a pixie. "Who are you?"

"My name's Dickory Dawdle," said the little fellow.

"How funny!" said Dicky. "Mine's Dicky Dawdle. Where do you live?"

"In Pixie Wood," said Dickory. "I say, come along and spend the night with me, and I'll take you to the Brownies' Circus tomorrow. It's very, very good. You'll love it! And if there's time we'll go to the Wise Gnome's party!"

"Oooh!" said Dicky, excited. "I'll go and ask my mother."

His mother said yes, he might go. So Dicky packed his nightclothes and his toothbrush and sponge and went to find Dickory again.

Together they went down the lane,

through a hole in the hedge, over a stile that Dicky had never seen before – and there they were in Pixie Wood! It was a most exciting place, for fairies, pixies and gnomes trotted about everywhere, going to market, chatting to one another, and popping in and out of tree-houses and toadstool cottages.

"We'll go to bed early, Dicky," said Dickory. "You see, we must catch the eight o'clock bus if we want to get to High-Up Hill, where the circus is held, in good time to buy front seats."

It was all very fine Dickory saying that – but he took such a long time getting the supper that Dicky was half asleep before it was finished!

Dickory Dawdle had a nice little house in a tree, with two round rooms – a sitting-room and a bedroom, one above the other. He *was* a dawdler! He would get the cloth to lay the table, and then put it down on a chair to do something else and forget all about the cloth.

Then he would spend half an hour hunting in the drawer again to find the

cloth. Dicky got quite cross with him.

Supper was lovely. It was chocolate pudding with ice-cream sauce, and ginger-beer to drink through long straws. But Dickory Dawdle was so long serving out the pudding that the ice-cream sauce melted into custard!

They finished their supper at last, and Dickory Dawdle got up to clear away. But he dawdled about so much that the table was still uncleared in half an hour's time, and Dicky began to do it himself. He was so sleepy by this time that he longed to go to bed.

"Do hurry up, Dickory," he said. "I never knew anyone so slow as you!"

"Oh yes, you know someone *just* as slow," said Dickory crossly. "*You* are a real dawdler, too. I knew it as soon as I saw you mooning along the lane, just looking at nothing! I wouldn't have asked you to spend the night with me if I'd thought you were going to be impatient. Go to bed if you want to!"

So Dicky undressed and got into the tiny bed that Dickory showed him. Dickory spent such a long time finding his pyjamas and dawdling round the room that Dicky was asleep long before Dickory was even in bed!

Dicky had a watch. He looked at it

when he woke up. He didn't want to miss the bus that went to High-Up Hill, for he badly wanted to see the Brownies' Circus.

"Hey, Dickory, it's seven o'clock already!" said Dicky. He jumped out of bed. This was a marvellous thing for him to do without being told, for he was usually very lazy indeed in the mornings!

Dickory didn't stir. Dicky pushed and shook him. "Leave me alone," said Dickory. "There's plenty of time."

"Well, we've got to dress and have breakfast," said Dicky impatiently. "I'll pull you out of bed!"

He did – and then Dickory *had* to get up, though he was very sulky about it. And, dear me, *how* he dawdled! He put a sock on – and then he sat on the bed and dreamed for a while. Then he put on another sock. After that he wandered round the room, whistling. Dicky watched him, feeling cross.

"Do hurry, Dickory. I want some breakfast before we go."

"Well, set the table then," said Dickory. "There is some cold ham in the larder, and we'll have ginger beer to drink again. It's too much bother to make tea or cocoa."

So Dicky had to get the breakfast, because he could quite well see that Dickory would never have time.

And then Dickory dawdled over breakfast! He took ten minutes to chew one mouthful of ham! Dicky got crosser and crosser, quite forgetting that this was the sort of thing he usually did himself every day.

They left the dirty breakfast things on the table and went to catch the bus. But Dickory wouldn't hurry a bit. He said there was plenty of time. He put his hands in his pockets and dawdled along, thinking of all kinds of things.

And when they got to the bus stop, in the middle of the wood, the bus was gone! There it was in the distance, a dear little yellow bus full of fairies and elves going to the circus! Dicky could have cried with rage.

"It's all your silly fault!" he said to Dickory. "If you hadn't been so slow over everything we would easily have caught the bus."

"Well, you're a fine fellow to talk, I must say!" said Dickory in surprise. "I've always heard that you are very slow yourself. Didn't I hear that you were late for school every day last week?"

Dicky went red. It was quite true. He and Dickory went back to the tree-house without saying a word more. They washed up, and then Dicky asked about the Gnome's party.

"What time do we have to be there?" he said.

"Half-past two," said Dickory firmly. "All dawdlers like forty winks and snoozes and naps. Now don't start shouting at me or hurrying me, because I just won't have it. I'm a dawdler, like you, and I WON'T BE HURRIED!"

Well, they didn't have dinner at twelve, because Dickory dawdled so much over the potatoes that they were not cooked till one. There were stewed apples and custard, too, and cold chicken, but as Dickory forgot to watch the custard cooking it got burnt and he had to make some more. So it was about one o'clock when they sat down to dinner.

And though Dicky ate quickly, with his eyes on the cuckoo-clock that hung on the wall, Dickory would *not* hurry himself. He dawdled over his chicken, he dawdled over his pudding. Dicky was nearly in despair.

"We shall be late for the party!" he said.

"Plenty of time, plenty of time," said Dickory, yawning. "We *must* have a snooze first." And the tiresome little fellow lay down on the couch and went straight off to sleep.

At a quarter-past two there was a knock on the tree-door. As Dickory was asleep, Dicky opened the door. There was a small fairy outside, very smartly dressed, all ready for the party. She smiled at Dicky.

"The rabbit carriage is here to take you and Dickory to the party," she said. "We are all waiting for you."

"Dickory's asleep!" cried Dicky, and he ran to shake the pixie. The fairy looked upset.

"We can't wait whilst you wash and tidy yourselves," she said. "And you can't possibly come like that. Look at your coat, Dickory! You've spilt custard all down it! You're such a dawdler that it would take you ages to change it. We shan't wait for you. Goodbye!"

"Oh, but can't you take me without Dickory?" asked Dicky, disappointed.

"Oh no!" said the fairy. "Come another time, but don't get Dawdle to take you or you'll never get there!"

She ran off. Dicky was very angry with Dickory. He put on his cap and went to the door.

"I'm going home," he said. "I'll never get anywhere if I leave things to you. You dreadful slowcoach!"

"Now just stop calling me names!" said Dickory angrily as he at last rose slowly from the couch. "Who's a slow old snail and never finishes his dinner until it's time for afternoon school? *You* are! Who's as slow as a tortoise over going to bed each night? *You* are!"

But Dicky wouldn't listen to any

more. It was dreadful to hear things like that – because he knew they were true.

"Well, if that's what it's like living with a dawdler, no wonder Mummy gets angry with *me*," said Dicky as he hurried home. "It seems as if dawdlers miss all the good things and all the treats. My word, Mummy's going to get a surprise tomorrow!"

And she did! You should have seen how Dicky jumped out of bed when he was called! You should have seen him run to school! And before the morning had gone he was top of the class.

Do you dawdle? Well, go and spend a day with Dickory Dawdle and tell me how you like it!

Think Hard, Boatman

Splash, the ferryman lived in a tiny house beside the river. He had a cheerful-looking little boat painted blue and the oars were orange. The boat was called *Here-we-go!* and everyone liked going across the river in it.

Splash was really a very busy little man. He took the postman across to deliver letters to the farms on the other side of the water. He took old Mrs Dumble to and fro every day when she went shopping. He took four children over and back each day too, because they went to Dame Little's School up the hill.

He sang as he rowed his boat to and fro:

Think Hard, Boatman

Over the river and back I go,
My little bright oars a-flashing,
Watch me ferrying to and fro,
Here-we-go, here-we-go, splashing!

When he sang the word "splashing" he dashed the oars hard into the water and made a terrific splash. Everyone liked that very much except old Mrs Dumble, who said that it made her jump and wetted her shawl.

Splash never refused to take anyone. Even when Mighty-One the wizard came, he didn't say no, though he shivered and shook all the time in case the wizard might suddenly work a spell

and take the boat off to the moon, or some other peculiar place.

And when Fat-One, the giant, wanted to be rowed across the river, even then Splash didn't say no! But he was so afraid the giant would weigh down the boat too much at his end that he put a big stone just beside his own seat, so that the boat wouldn't tip too much.

It made the rowing very hard, because the boat was heavy then, with the giant and the stone. Still, somehow Splash managed, and he made it quite a boast that he had never said no to anyone who wanted to go across the river, or wanted goods rowed across to the other side.

But wait a minute! There was a time when Splash very nearly *did* say no! It was when old Witch Grim told him she was going to leave him some goods to take across for her. Splash didn't know what the goods were, but he didn't like the sound of them.

"You've got to be careful with my goods," the witch said. "If any get

damaged I shall make you pay, Splash. In fact, I might even take your boat away!"

"When will you leave the goods to be taken across?" asked Splash. "And what are they?"

"Two animals and a nice big bag of carrots," said Witch Grim. "Mr Quick will bring them in his cart this evening."

Well, when Mr Quick came with his cart, Splash happened to be the other side of the river with old Mrs Dumble. Mr Quick hailed him loudly.

"Hey, Splash! Here are the goods from Witch Grim. I can't wait, so hurry

up and fetch them before they damage one another."

Splash rowed back as fast as he could, and there, waiting for him on the other side, were the goods.

One red fox, all alive-oh!

One white rabbit, scared of the fox.

One bag of carrots that made the rabbit feel very hungry indeed.

"Well now!" said Splash, scratching his head and looking at the goods. "I can't possibly take more than one of you across at once. You'd be too heavy for me, because I'm tired now. Which shall I take first?"

"Take me!" said the rabbit. "I'm scared of the fox. Take me, Mr Splash, and leave me safely on the other side. Then row back and get the carrots."

"Right," said Splash. Then he stopped and scratched his head again. "Ah, but wait a minute! If I take you across – and then fetch the bag of carrots and leave it with you, you'll nibble the lot! I know you, Rabbit!"

"Well, take the rabbit across, and then take me, and take the carrots last," said the fox.

"Right," said the boatman. But the rabbit gave a loud squeal.

"Oh, no Mr Splash! If you do that you will have to leave the fox alone with me on the other side whilst you go back for the carrots – and he'll eat me!"

"Take me across first then," said the fox.

"Aha – and leave the carrots and the rabbit together on this side!" said Splash. "Not if I know it, Red Fox!"

"Well, what are you going to do then?" said the red fox. "Either the rabbit and I are left together on one side or the other, or the rabbit and the carrots."

Splash sat down on a tree-stump and scratched his head again. He thought very hard indeed. He simply must not leave rabbit and fox together, or rabbit and carrots. The fox would eat the rabbit, the rabbit would eat the carrots – and then Witch Grim would be very angry and take his boat away.

The red fox sat down too and grinned at Splash. "It's no good," he said. "Work it out how you will, Splash, *something's* going to be eaten. And *you're* going to get into trouble!"

Think hard, boatman! Think hard! There's a way to do it, if only you'll think hard.

What, you don't think there is? Think again. Yes, Splash, you can do it, and nothing will be eaten, but just think hard and find out how!

Splash thought so hard that his eyes disappeared under an enormous frown. Then he jumped up and smacked his hands together loudly. The fox and rabbit jumped.

"I know how to do it!" said Splash.

"You don't," said the fox, disappointed.

"I do!" said Splash. "Rabbit, get into the boat! You're the first to go across."

The rabbit got in, looking very doubtful. Splash rowed him across to the other side and left him there. He rowed back to where he had left the fox and the carrots. He popped the carrots into his boat and rowed back to the rabbit.

"Hey!" called the fox. "The rabbit will eat the carrots if you leave them over there with him."

But Splash didn't mean to do that. Oh no! he threw out the bag of carrots and called to the surprised rabbit to get back into the boat again – and he rowed him back to the fox!

Think Hard, Boatman

"Now get out," he said to the rabbit, "and you, Red Fox, get in! I'm leaving you on this side again for a bit, Rabbit. I'll be back to fetch you soon."

He rowed the fox across to where he had left the carrots and made him get out. "The carrots will be safe enough with *you!*" he said. "Now I'm off to get the rabbit!"

And back he went to get the rabbit. He rowed him over to the fox and the carrots. "There!" he said. "I've done it – and nothing's eaten! And here comes Witch Grim to fetch you all! Hey, Witch Grim, my fee, please!"

"What! You managed to get these goods across safely!" said Witch Grim. "Splash, you're very, very clever. I quite expected either the rabbit or the carrots would be eaten!"

Splash *was* clever, wasn't he? Would *you* have thought of that way, do you think?

64

The Dirty Old Hat

Once Flibberty went to have a cup of tea in Dame Trotty's tea-room. It was crowded with people, for Dame Trotty made lovely buns and biscuits.

Flibberty sat down, after he had hung his hat up on the peg behind him. He ordered tea and cakes, and enjoyed his tea very much.

Then he stood up, took down what he thought was his hat from the peg behind, and went out. But it wasn't his hat. It was the Little Enchanter's hat and it was a magic one. It looked dirty and old, but it was crammed full of magic.

Flibberty put the hat on and went out, humming. He wished it wasn't such a long way home. He looked down at his shoes and sighed.

"You're uncomfortable shoes," he said. "You're too small. I wish I had lovely, red ones, like the ones Prince Twinkle has."

To his enormous astonishment his old shoes disappeared, and he saw on his feet a pair of fine, red leather ones. Flibberty couldn't believe his eyes!

"Look at that now!" he said. "A pair of new shoes – and all for the wishing! There must be something magic about me today!"

He stood still and thought for a moment. Then he wished again. "I'd like a red cloak like Prince Twinkle's, too," he said. And at once a red cloak swung out from his shoulders! Flibberty was so delighted he couldn't say a word for quite two minutes.

"I'm grand!" he said. "Red shoes and red cloak! Would you believe it! I'll wish for a few more things!"

He wished for a stick with a gold handle. It came into his hand at once. Marvellous!

"This wishing business is a very good thing!" said Flibberty, pleased. "I'll have a new suit now – gold and silver, please, with shining buttons all the way down!" It came, of course! Flibberty really did look very grand now. He thought he would like a carriage of his own.

"I know what I'll do! I'll wish for a carriage and go and call on Gibberty in it!" he said. Gibberty was his friend. They lived together. How surprised Gibberty would be to see Flibberty arriving in a carriage, all dressed up like a prince!

"I wish for a carriage!" said Flibberty. One appeared at once – but it was too small for Flibberty and had no horses.

"I wish for a *big* carriage, and twelve white horses," he said grandly. They were there! The white horses pawed the ground and one of them neighed.

"They're absolutely real!" said Flibberty. He climbed up into the coachman's seat and then decided that there were too many horses for him to drive. So he got down and climbed into the carriage instead. Then he wished for two coachmen and two footmen. "I'll have them dressed in red and silver," he said.

They appeared, dressed in red and silver. Flibberty couldn't help feeling delighted with himself. He hoped he would meet plenty of people on the way home. Wouldn't they stare to see him in his lovely carriage with coachmen and footmen!

"I'll have some dogs, too," he suddenly thought. "I like dogs. I'll have about a hundred, and they can run behind the carriage."

"I wish for a hundred dogs, please," he said out loud. The dogs appeared. They

seemed very well-behaved. They didn't jump up and try to lick Flibberty. They put themselves behind the carriage, and not one of them barked.

Flibberty half-thought he would have some cats as well, just to make a sensation, but he decided he wouldn't. It might make the dogs ill-behaved if he made cats run with them.

"And now I think I'll have a sack of gold pieces and throw them out as I go along," thought Flibberty. "That would be a kind and princely thing to do! I wish for a sack of gold!" It appeared on the seat beside him. Ah, that was fine. Now he would drive slowly along to his house, and

wouldn't he enjoy seeing Gibberty's face when he came to the door!

"Drive on!" he commanded the coachmen, and on they drove. The horses' hooves made a tremendous noise, clip-clopping along. People came out to see them. When they saw the beautiful carriage and horses, and all the dogs following behind, they stared as if they couldn't believe their eyes!

They didn't even recognise Flibberty! He bowed and smiled to them, but not one of them guessed this grand prince to be the little Flibberty they knew so well. He put his hand into the sack and drew out a dozen gold pieces. He threw them to the delighted people.

"This will make them rich!" thought

Flibberty, pleased. "There's old Dame Crick — she's picked up three gold pieces! My, my, won't she be glad!"

Soon he arrived at his cottage. Gibberty, hearing the noise of the horses, came running out. He didn't recognise Flibberty at all. He bowed very low indeed.

"Gibberty! It's me, Flibberty!" said his friend with a chuckle. Gibberty looked up in great astonishment. Yes — it *was* Flibberty. Well, well, well!

"Whatever's happened to you?" said Gibberty.

"I don't know," said Flibberty. "It must be my lucky day, I should think. Everything I wish for comes true. It's marvellous."

71

"Well, wish something for *me*, quick!" said Gibberty.

"Wait a bit, wait a bit! Don't rush me so," said Flibberty. "You haven't admired my twelve white horses and my hundred dogs."

"I can't imagine why you wished for a hundred dogs," said Gibberty, who wasn't very fond of dogs. "I don't know how we're going to feed them, or where they'll live."

"I shall wish them magnificent kennels and stacks of the most wonderful food," said Flibberty.

"Well, wish some wonderful food for me this very minute," said Gibberty. "I'm hungry! Come on, Flibberty, use some of your magic for *me!*"

"I'll wish you a fine suit of clothes, like mine," said Flibberty.

"Well, don't wish me a hat like yours!" said Gibberty. "I never saw such a dirty old thing in my life! Why don't you wish for a new one?"

Flibberty took his hat off his head and looked at it in surprise. "It's not mine,"

he said. "What a dirty old hat! How disgusting! I shan't wear it. I shall throw it away!" He threw it high in the air. It caught on a tree – and just as it left Flibberty's hand, everything that he had wished for disappeared! His new clothes went, his carriage, horses, servants and dogs! Nothing was left at all!

"They've gone!" said Flibberty. "Oh, you silly, stupid creature, Gibberty! The magic must have been in that hat! Quick, we must get it down from that tree." But before they could get it down the Little Enchanter came hurrying along to get it. He had heard of Flibberty's good luck and had guessed what had happened! Flibberty had taken his hat by mistake.

The Dirty Old Hat

"That's *my* hat!" he roared, and he threw Flibberty's at him. "Here's yours. You leave my hat alone! If you've used up all the magic in it I'll turn you into a scrubbing-brush and use you for spring-cleaning!"

"Ooooh!" squealed Flibberty and Gibberty and they tore indoors. But luckily Flibberty hadn't used all the magic, and the Little Enchanter put his hat firmly on his head and strode off home.

"To think I wore a wishing-hat and didn't know it but threw it away!" groaned Flibberty. "Next time I'll be a lot more careful!"

I daresay he will – but there won't *be* a next time!

Freddie
Has a Job

Next door to Freddie there lived an old man who couldn't walk. He lay on a couch by his window all day long, and looked out into his garden. His name was Mr Still, and Freddie used to think it was a good name for anyone who had to lie still all day long.

The old man liked to see his flowers in the spring and summer. He had crocuses in the early spring, and then hundreds of golden daffodils nodding in the March wind. Then he had tulips, and after that a crowd of flowers — lupins, irises, sweet-williams, roses — everything you could think of.

He often smiled at Freddie when he saw him looking over the wall. "Good morning!" he would call. "A nice day for the roses – and for little boys too!"

When the autumn came, and all the flowers died except the big clumps of Michaelmas daisies, Mr Still got his housekeeper to put up a big bird-table. Then he watched that instead of his flowers. He used to have crumbs, seeds, soaked dog-biscuits, scrapings of pudding, and all kinds of things put on the table – and, dear me, you should have seen the number of birds that came to feast there!

Freddie could see the bird-table from his bedroom window. "Look, Mother!" he said each morning. "Look at all the sparrows – and there are two robins – and lots of greedy starlings – and a chaffinch and blackbird and a thrush."

Freddie Has a Job

It was fun to watch them all, but Mother wouldn't let him stay in his cold bedroom for long. She made him come down to the warm sitting-room and play there. He couldn't see the bird-table from there.

"Mother, couldn't *I* have a bird-table too?" asked Freddie. "I would so love to have one."

"No, you can't," said Mother. "They are too expensive to buy, and I can't make one."

"I think *I* could," said Freddie. "All I want is a piece of flat wood for the top, and a long stick of some kind for the leg. That's all, Mother."

But Mother said no. And as she meant no when she said no, it wasn't any good asking her again.

Freddie watched the bird-table being taken down in the spring. Mr Still always said that he expected the birds to return his kindness then, and eat the greenfly and the caterpillars in his garden, so that his flowers would be as lovely as possible. The daffodils were beginning to flower. It was time for the birds to begin hunting for caterpillars!

The summer went by, and Mr Still's garden was more beautiful than ever – especially the roses; but when the autumn came, Freddie was most surprised to see that no bird-table was put up as usual! He looked from his bedroom window each morning as he dressed, but no – there was no bird-table there. Freddie wondered why.

So one morning he climbed up and sat on the wall between the two gardens. He called to Mr Still, who lay on his couch as usual by the window.

"Mr Still! Have you forgotten your bird-table this autumn? The birds come hopping round, looking for it, but you haven't had it put up."

Mr Still pushed open the window and nodded to Freddie. "No, I haven't forgotten it," he said. "But you see, Freddie, things are difficult now, so every scrap of bread is used up, and I mustn't even buy dog-biscuits, because it is not right to give them to the birds when there is only just enough for our dogs. All the milk-puddings we have are scraped round for us to finish up ourselves, instead of giving them to the birds."

"Oh I see," said Freddie, sadly. "Mr Still, won't the birds be awfully disappointed? They keep looking for your bird-table, you know. Can't you put berries or seeds on it?"

"I could, if only my legs would take me into the fields and lanes to collect berries and wild seeds," said Mr Still.

"But they won't walk, you know, Freddie. Something is wrong with them, and they can't be cured. I am just as disappointed as the birds about the bird-table – I did so love watching them. There isn't much for me to do here, and I do miss seeing my little feathered friends on the table."

"Well," said Freddie, suddenly thinking of a good idea, "well, Mr Still – let *me* be your legs! Why can't *I* go off into the fields and lanes and pick berries and seeds for the birds? Then you could have your table up, and watch the birds just as usual!"

"Would you really do that for me?" said Mr Still, smiling. "That's very kind of you indeed. If you would come to tea with me today I could tell you all the berries and seeds to get!"

So Freddie went to tea, and he and Mr Still talked about what to get for the bird-table. The next day was Saturday, so Freddie was able to go off to collect what he could find.

He did have fun. He found those

lovely bright scarlet hips that grow on the wild rose. He found masses of crimson hawthorn berries. He found purple privet berries, and plenty of yew berries too – though Mr Still said they were poisonous to little boys, so, although the birds loved them, Freddie mustn't eat them.

Freddie found plenty of seeds, too. He shook out old flower-heads into a paper bag, and tiny brown and black and yellow seeds rattled down into it from all kinds of plants.

"The birds will pick out those they want," said Mr Still. "They are very

sensible. They know which are bad for them and which are good."

Freddie saw some great sunflower heads growing in Mrs Brown's garden one day. She was just cutting them down, and Freddie called to her.

"Mrs Brown! Do you want all those sunflower seeds for next year? If you don't, may I have some for a bird-table?"

"Certainly," said Mrs Brown. "I'll just keep one or two heads and dry them. I shall want seed for sunflowers again, because I do love these giant sunflowers – and I always save some seed for my sister's old parrot. But you can have all the other heads if you like!"

Wasn't Freddie pleased! There were seven big heads, full of fat sunflower seeds! He took them to Mr Still.

"Splendid!" said the old man. "We will dry them and then hang them up

one by one from the bird-table, so that the birds can peck them as they please. They *will* have a feast!"

Freddie found acorns and chopped them up to put on the bird-table. He found hazelnuts and chopped those up too, or threaded the shelled nuts on string for the tits, who loved them.

"Well, really, I don't think I've ever seen my bird-table so full before!" said Mr Still, watching the crowd of birds hopping on it. "It's marvellous. I don't know what I should have done without you, Freddie. I do hope you get some pleasure out of watching the table, too!"

"Well, I don't really see it much, though I should simply love to," said Freddie. "You see, I can only see it from my window when I'm dressing. I can't see it from downstairs. I do wish I had one of my own – but Mother said no, and I can't bother her about it again."

"No, of course not,"said Mr Still. "Well, I can tell you I *have* had fun this winter watching the birds gobble up all the seeds and berries and nuts you have found for them."

The next week was Christmas week. Freddie was very busy making presents for everyone, and he hadn't much time to go hunting for berries and seeds – but it didn't matter, because he and Mr Still had a good store now, drying in a shed, ready to use if snow came and covered the trees and bushes.

Freddie gave Mr Still a present. It was a calendar he had made himself,

with a picture of two robins on it. Mr Still was very pleased indeed.

"Thank you," he said. "My present for you will be coming along soon. It may have two robins on it too, but I can't promise that!"

Freddie wondered what the present would be, and when Christmas morning came, he looked carefully through his presents to find Mr Still's. And he was very disappointed indeed not to find one! He thought Mr Still must have forgotten him after all.

But he hadn't – for when Freddie came downstairs and looked out of the window, what do you think he saw? He saw a fine big bird-table standing in his own garden, just near the window-sill, so that he could see it, and from it hung a large label that said, "For Freddie – from Mr Still and all the birds, with love and twitters and chirrups!"

"Oh!" cried Freddie joyfully. "A bird-table of my own! The finest one I've ever seen! Oh, Mother, I'm so happy!"

"You deserve to be, Freddie," said his

mother, smiling at him. "And do look at your first visitors."

Sure enough, two robins flew down to the new bird-table and looked at Freddie as if to say, "Breakfast, please!" They were just like the ones on the calendar that Freddie had given to Mr Still. It was really very strange. He rushed in to tell Mr Still.

"Well, now you *will* be busy," said the old man, smiling. "You will have *two* bird-tables to spread each day with food and water. What a fine thing it was that you thought of going out to get berries and seeds!"

And don't forget, will you, that *you* can spread a bird-table with the same things, even if you have very few crumbs or potatoes or scrapings to spare. It's such fun hunting in the woods and fields for bird-food. You'll love it.

A Visitor
to Dinner

Keith and Penny were very fond of the birds. In the spring they put out lucky-bags for them – net bags full of dead leaves, moss, hair and feathers so that the birds could come and take what they wanted for their nests. In the summer they put out bowls of water for the birds to bathe in and drink.

And when the cold weather came they had a bird-table, of course. Keith had made it himself.

"I think it's a very good table, Keith," said Penny. "I know it's only a flat bit of wood nailed on top of a pole, with twigs nailed at the back for the birds to perch on when they fly down – but you've made it very strongly, and the birds really do love it."

So they did. The sparrows were always there, of course. The robin came by himself, and wouldn't let any other robin near the table. The blackbirds came and the thrushes, and the little chaffinches flew down to it a dozen times a day.

"There are always plenty of guests at your table!" Mother said to them. "Whenever I look out of the window I see some bird or other pecking away there."

"Yes – and the robin still likes to bathe in the little dish of water," said Penny, "although the winter is here and the days are cold. He splashes in the water as if it were summer!"

So he did – and the thrush sometimes had a bathe too, though he was really too big for the little dish. The children were always thinking of things to put

on their bird-table for their visitors to
eat. They really were very good friends
to them.

They put out all the crumbs, of
course, and the scrapings from every
pudding. They put out the skins of
potatoes that had been boiled in their
jackets, and once a week Mother baked
two potatoes specially for the birds.
Keith and Penny cut them in half, let
them cool, and then put the four halves
on the table.

"You should see the birds fight for
the potato, Mother!" said Penny. "They
simply love it. Have you a bone we can
have for the starlings? They were down
there on the table today, and they do so
like a bone."

So Mother gave them a bone and
the starlings flew down and squabbled
over it as they always did. They called

each other rude names and pushed one another off the bone. They really were very funny.

"What birds come to your table?" asked Daddy, one evening. "Anything exciting? When I kept a table a nut-hatch once came to it for nuts I put there – he was a beauty. He whistled as the paper-boy does."

"Did he really?" said Penny. "I wish we had some uncommon bird visitors – but we never do. We get the sparrows and chaffinches, the blackbirds and thrushes, the robins and the starlings."

"And the tits," said Keith. "Don't

forget them. We hung a piece of fat meat on a bit of string yesterday, Daddy, and the blue tits came and swung on the string like acrobats!"

"But one tit was the cleverest of the lot," said Penny. "He stood on the edge of the table and hauled the fat up to him! I could hardly believe my eyes."

"Very clever," said Daddy. "But those are all quite common birds. Perhaps one of these days you will get a rare one."

All the birds in that district knew Keith and Penny, and their bird-table. The sparrows chattered about them, the chaffinches told the two bullfinches that lived in the hedgerow, and tried to make them come to the table, and the song-thrush told his big cousin, the mistlethrush.

"I'll come to the children's table after Christmas," said the mistlethrush. "Perhaps they will put out their mistletoe sprays for me then, and I can peck off the mistletoe berries. I do like them so much."

Then one day a ripple of excitement

ran through the bird-world in that district. "Have you seen the Big-Beaked One? Have you seen him? He is enormous!"

Sparrows told the news to chaffinches, blackbirds called to peewits up in the sky, and the peewits told the rooks and jackdaws.

"There's a great bird in the fields – he's called the Big-Beaked One!" all the birds cried. "Nobody knows where he comes from."

"What does he eat?" called the kingfisher.

"He's like you – he wants fish," said the blackbird. "But he says the little fish you catch are no use to him – he wants big fish to fill his beak!"

The birds went to see this strange visitor. They stared at him in awe. Truly he was big and truly he had a big beak – an enormous one, which would surely take twenty fish at a time! The big bird was not very friendly. He would not say where he had come from nor what his real name was. He sat by the riverside where the kingfisher fished, and grumbled because the fish were so small.

"I am hungry," he said. "I am always hungry. Are you not hungry too, thrushes, blackbirds and sparrows?"

"No," piped up a sparrow, "we know where there is always a table spread with good things for us."

Big-Beaked One listened hard. "A table spread with good things?" he said. "Is there fish?"

"I've never seen any," said the sparrow. "But Keith and Penny, the two children who always spread the table for us each day, will be sure to get you

fish if you want some. They are very, very kind."

"Then show me where this table is," said Big-Beaked One, and he flapped his great wings and made such a wind that the sparrow was blown right off his twig.

It was the blackbird who took him to the table. "There you are," he said. "I'm afraid the table is not large enough for a bird like you – but if you sit right in the middle of it you'll have room."

And that afternoon for the first time Keith and Penny caught sight of the strange and unexpected visitor! They stared in the greatest astonishment.

"Are we dreaming?" said Keith. "Can you see a most enormous bird on our table, Penny?"

"Yes – and oh, Keith – it looks like a *pelican* to me!" said Penny, amazed.

"A pelican – why, I believe you are right!" said Keith. "He's certainly got a pelican's funny beak – very big indeed, with a pouch to hold fish. But where has he come from?"

"There aren't any pelicans in *this* country," said Penny. "Are we dreaming?"

"No. That bird looks much too real for a dream," said Keith. "It *is* a pelican! Why has it come?"

"For us to feed it, of course," said Penny. "I expect it's hungry, poor thing, and the other birds have told it to come to our table. We must give it food."

"Yes – that's all very well – but it won't eat bread or cake or anything like that," said Keith. "Pelicans live on fish!"

"Then we'll go and buy some fish from the fishmonger's," said Penny. "That's easy. I'll go and tell Mother and ask her for some money."

But Mother was out. So the children took their own money-boxes and emptied them. They looked doubtfully at the money. "Do you think it's enough?" said Penny. "The pelican looks as if it could eat up an awful lot of fish."

"It'll have to be enough," said Keith. "It's all we've got. Come on, we'd better go and buy the fish before the pelican gets tired of waiting."

Penny called out of the window. "Pelican! Welcome to our bird-table. We're sorry there's no fish, but we didn't know you were coming. We're just going to get some for you!"

The pelican looked at them out of his artful-looking eyes. He nodded his head slowly. "There! I'm sure he understood," said Penny. The children ran to their front gate and down the road. They were soon at the fishmonger's.

"What fish do you want?" asked the man.

"Have you anything fit for pelicans?" asked Keith.

The fishmonger laughed.

"Don't be funny," he said. "I'm busy. What fish do you want? And don't tell me you want something for an ostrich this time."

"No, we don't," said Penny. "It really is for a pelican."

The fishmonger lost patience with them. "I've no time to joke about pelicans," he said. "Here, take some herrings. I've got plenty of those."

The pelican was still on their table, waiting patiently. "I wonder if he'll take them from us," said Keith. He held out a herring and the pelican snapped at it at once! It took one from Penny next.

"Isn't he tame!" said Keith. "What will Daddy say when we tell him we had a pelican visitor this afternoon?"

A Visitor to Dinner

Well, Daddy simply didn't believe it, of course. He laughed. "Don't try to kid me with pelican tales," he said. "I'll believe in the pelican when I see him!"

"You'll see him tomorrow, perhaps," said Penny. "He liked the fish we gave him today, so I expect he'll come back."

Well, he did! He arrived the very next morning and sat solidly in the middle of the bird-table, waiting, much to the annoyance of the sparrows and other small birds who hadn't any room to perch at all!

"There he is, Daddy – *now* will you believe us?" asked Keith. Daddy went to the window. He stared in silence. Then he spoke in surprise.

"Well! It is a pelican. He's escaped from somewhere, of course. Perhaps from the Zoo. I'll ring them up and see."

So he rang up the Zoo – and they said yes, Percy the Pelican had escaped. Was he *really* on the children's bird-table?

"Yes. The children are giving him fish," said Daddy. "Can you send a keeper down? I think you could catch him easily if he visits us again."

That afternoon a keeper arrived from the Zoo. He carried a big long- handled net with him. He hid behind a bush and waited.

When Percy flew down, the children went to the table to give him fish – and down over him came the keeper's net. He was caught!

The keeper took him back to the Zoo. The children were very sorry, because they liked Percy. "All the same he would have been expensive to feed," said Penny. "We've already spent all

the money we've saved up for Mummy's birthday, worse luck!" But that didn't matter after all – because by the next day's post there came a letter from the Zoo – and in it was five pounds for Keith and five pounds for Penny.

"Just to pay for Percy's board and lodging," said the note.

"We'll *never* have such an unusual visitor again," said Keith. "Fancy having Percy the Pelican to dinner! I'm sure nobody else ever has."

But I'd like to. Wouldn't you?

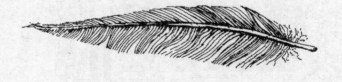

The Smugglers' Caves

Bill and David were staying at their grandmother's, down by the sea.

They were very excited because Grandpa had been telling them about the old smugglers' caves round by the big cliff.

"Oh, Grandpa! Could we explore them, do you think? Should we find anything there – you know, left by the old smugglers?" asked Bill.

Grandpa laughed. "No! You'll find nothing but sand and shells and seaweed," he said. "There have been plenty of people in and out of those caves year after year. If there was anything to be found, it would have been found by now!"

"Still, it would be fun to explore them," said David. "We could pretend we were smugglers. Come on, Bill — we'll go this morning!"

Off they went, running down the road to the big, sandy beach, and then round the sand to where the big cliffs stuck out, steep and rocky. In these were the caves.

"Oh, look — there's a whole lot of Boy Scouts on the beach," said Bill. "Gosh I wish I was old enough to be a Scout. They have such fun. I bet they're going to camp somewhere here for a week or two, and bathe, and picnic, and hike all day long! Do you think they'd let us be with them sometimes?" But when the two small boys came near the company of Scouts they didn't get much of a welcome.

"You clear off, you kids," said one of the big boys. "This is our part of the beach, see? Don't you make yourselves nuisances here."

The small boys went off, disappointed. "They could just have let us *watch* their games," said Bill. "We wouldn't have been a nuisance. We could even have run after their balls for them, if they went too far."

"Oh, never mind – let's go and look for the caves," said David. "I'd rather explore them than watch boys who think we're too small to be anything but nuisances."

"Here's a cave," said Bill, and he went up to where a dark hole yawned at the foot of the cliff. "It's a big one. Let's go in."

They went into it. The floor was of soft sand, and seaweed hung down the

sides of the walls. The sea went in and out at high tide and filled the little pools at the sides of the cave.

"It's a nice cave, but not very exciting," said Bill. "I don't feel as if smugglers ever came in here, do you, David? Anyway, it doesn't lead anywhere. I mean, there are no inner caves or tunnels leading into the cliff."

"Let's find another cave," said David. So off they went to the next one. But that was very small, and they could hardly stand upright in it. They went out again into the sunshine.

Then they noticed a stretch of rugged rocks leading up to another cave in the cliff – a cave that really did look exciting. It had quite a small entrance. The boys climbed up the rocks to it and peered inside.

"It's nice and dark," said Bill. "Got your torch, David? We'll need it here."

David switched on his torch. The boys made their way inside the cave. It was really more like a big tunnel, and it led to an inner cave. David shone his torch

round. Then he gave a sudden shout.

"Bill! What's that over there? Look!"

Bill looked over to the corner into which David's torch shone. Well hidden, there were what looked like sacks and boxes. Gracious! Had they suddenly hit on some old smugglers' stores after all?

"Make sure those Boy Scouts aren't anywhere about," said David. "We don't want them to interfere in this. This is *our* discovery, see?"

Bill went to the outer entrance of the tunnel-like cave. He peered out. No, there were no boys about. But wait a bit

– wasn't the sea a good bit nearer now?

He called to David. "Hey! I think the tide's coming in pretty fast. Will it reach these caves, do you think? We don't want to be caught."

"Yes. I think it *will* reach them – and then we shall be stuck here for hours," said David. "Blow! Just as we have found treasure, too! I don't like going off and leaving it here, with all those Scouts about. They're pretty certain to come nosing round these caves, and then they'll find it, too."

"Well, we can't possibly take all these sacks and things down the beach with us," said Bill. "Won't it be all right to leave them here, David?"

"No. If *we* can find them, somebody else easily can!" said David. "I'm surprised nobody has spotted them before. I know what we'll do, Bill."

"What?" said Bill.

"We'll drag them to that place halfway up the cave wall," said David, pointing. "Do you see, there's a kind of big hole there? It may have been a proper hidy-hole once for smuggled things. I think we could drag everything up there and hide it well. We could drape some seaweed over the hole."

It was difficult to drag everything up to the hole. The boys did not stop to open the sacks or boxes, for they were so afraid of being cut off by the tide. They managed to drag them into the hole at last, and then they hastily arranged big fronds of seaweed over the 'treasure' to hide it. When they had finished they

were sure no one could possibly see it.

They slid down to the cave floor. They went cautiously to the outer entrance and peered out. They would just have time to run round the edge of the cliff before the sea was swirling all round it!

"There are the Scouts, look – in the next cave but one!" said Bill. "I wonder what they want. They're yelling to each other rather crossly. Somebody's done something silly, I should think."

"Well come on – let's go before they yell at *us!*" said David. The two small boys ran round the foot of the cliff, wading through a shallow stretch of water in one place. They were only just

in time! The tide would soon be right up the cliff – and into some of those caves.

"The Scouts will get caught if they don't look out," said Bill.

"Oh, they're big enough to swim if they get caught by the tide," said David. "Or they might even dare to climb up the cliffs!"

They went home to dinner. They told Grandpa about their exciting find, but he only laughed.

"Go on with you!" he said. "Telling me you've found smugglers' treasure in those caves! Why, I've been in and out of them thousands of times when I was a boy. You don't suppose you could find what I didn't do you?"

"Well, but, Grandpa," said Bill, "we really and truly *did* find treasure. At least – we didn't open the sacks because we didn't have time – but what else could be in them but old forgotten treasure?" Grandpa just laughed again. It was most disappointing of him. The boys decided not to say any more. It spoilt things if grown-ups laughed at them.

After dinner they slipped out again, hoping that the tide would soon go down and that they could once more go to the cave – and, this time, undo the 'treasure' and see what they had got!

They waded round the foot of the cliffs and came to the stretch of rocks that led up to their cave. They were soon hauling the treasure out of its hidy-hole to the floor below. "It's a jolly good thing we put it up where we did or it would have got soaking wet," said Bill. "The sea came right into the cave!"

They began to open the sacks – but what a surprise they got! There was

no 'treasure'! One sack was full of cups and plates and knives and forks! Another one had tins of food in it, and big loaves of bread, and about three dozen buns! One of the boxes had cricket stumps and balls in! What a very extraordinary thing!

"This isn't smugglers' treasure!" said Bill in dismay. "But what is it? And why is it here? Who does it belong to?"

"I say – do you think it belongs to the

scouts?" said David in rather a small voice. "It's rather the sort of things they'd bring away to camp with them. I don't think we'd better undo any more."

The boys stared at one another in dismay and fright. Had they meddled with the Scouts' belongings? How *could* they have thought they had found smugglers' treasure when they knew the sea swept in and out of that cave! How silly of them. No wonder Grandpa had laughed.

They were disappointed and miserable. "We simply shan't dare to say a word about this to the Scouts," said Bill, his voice trembling. "They'd skin us alive!"

"Let's go before they discover us here with their things," said David. So they crept out of the cave and made their way along the foot of the cliffs again. And they bumped straight into a meeting of the Scouts!

"I tell you I *did* put the things into one of the caves!" a red-faced Scout was saying. "I did! Even if the sea had gone in, surely it wouldn't have swept *everything* out!"

"Well, not a single thing is there," said the Scout-leader. "And here we are, come to camp, with our food, crockery, knives and forks, everything gone! We were idiots to dump our things down like that. We should have set up camp and unpacked straight away instead of fooling about."

"I suppose there's nothing for it but to go back home," said another Scout, looking very blue.

Bill and David couldn't help hearing all this. They felt dreadful. It was their fault that the Scouts hadn't been able

to find their things – it would be their fault if they had to give up camping and go back home.

Bill pulled David. He was scared and wanted to get back home. But David was made of stronger stuff, and besides, he was older. He suddenly walked straight up to the Scout-leader, his face scarlet, and spoke to him.

"I'm awfully sorry – but we stuck your goods into a hidy-hole halfway up a cave-wall," he said. "A good thing we did, too, or they would have been soaked by the sea. You will find them in the cave quite safe."

"You wretched little nuisances!" cried a Scout. "You want a good telling off!"

"No, he doesn't," said the leader. "It was a jolly good thing he found our sacks and boxes and put them out of reach of the sea – and it can't have been an easy thing to walk up to us and confess it all, not knowing what we'd do to him. He's a good youngster, and I won't have him yelled at."

There was a bit of grumbling, but

nobody else shouted at Bill and David. "You come along and show me which cave the things are in," said the leader to David. "We seem to have forgotten even which cave we used!" Bill and David took the Scouts to the cave. They were pleased when they saw all their goods. "Now we can camp all right," said a tall Scout. "Thank goodness these kids had the sense to drag everything out of reach of the water."

"We thought it was smugglers'

treasure," explained Bill, with a red face. But the Scouts didn't laugh. The leader clapped him on the back.

"You'll make a good Scout one day," he said. "You ought to join the Cubs, you know, you and your brother. Would you like to watch us camping? You can come to breakfast tomorrow with us if you like."

Well, what do you think of that? The two boys beamed all over their faces.

"Oh, thanks a lot!" said David. "We promise not to make ourselves nuisances."

They didn't. They made themselves so useful that the Scout-leader said he really didn't know what they would do without them. And one night he even let them sleep in a tent with some of the others.

And now, as you can guess, Bill and David are both good Cubs. Are *you* a Cub or a Brownie? I'm sure you will be if you get the chance.

Patter's Adventure

In a hole in a bank at the bottom of Mary's garden lived a mouse family. They were long-tailed field-mice, pretty little things, and as playful as could be.

Every day the mother mouse ran off to get food for the family. She knew exactly where to get it. Mary kept two doves in a cage, and she fed them each day, sometimes with grain and sometimes with bread.

The mouse was small enough to creep under the big cage where the doves lived and take a piece of bread. Before the doves could peck her she was out again, running down the garden with the bread. Then the little mouse family would have a lovely feast.

Patter's Adventure

Now one day Patter, the youngest of the family, wanted an adventure. He had often heard his mother talk of the wonderful place where bread could always be found, and he wanted to see it for himself. So he followed his mother and saw where she went.

But as she came back she saw Patter. She dropped the bread at once and flew at him. "Patter! You bad, naughty little mouse! How dare you come out alone like this! Don't you know that Bubbles the cat is about?"

Patter had no idea what a cat was. He stared at his mother and his tiny nose went up and down. He curled his long tail round his little body and looked miserable.

"What's a cat?" he said.

"Oh, the baby! Fancy asking what a CAT is!" said his mother. "You'll know soon enough one day if you run about alone when you're no more than a few days old!"

She took Patter back and gave him such a talking-to that he didn't stir out of the nest for days. Then he suddenly felt that he must have an adventure again. And this time, he thought, he would go by himself right up to the doves' cage and find a bit of bread on his own. Then he could eat it all without having to share it with four brothers and sisters.

So off he went, a little tiny thing almost small enough to pop under a thimble!

Now Bubbles the cat had three

growing kittens. They were five weeks old and very playful. They rolled about, they climbed out of their basket, and they ran unsteadily over the kitchen floor. They often tried to catch their mother's tail.

"It is time you stopped being babies," said Bubbles one night. "You must learn what it is to hunt for mice. One day you will have to catch food for yourselves, and I must teach you."

"What are mice?" asked Ginger, who was the biggest kitten. Bubbles was astonished.

"What! You don't know what mice are! How ignorant you are! I will catch one and bring it in for you. You shall play with it, catch it for yourselves and eat it. Mice are very tasty."

So out Bubbles went, the same night

that Patter was off on his adventure. She knew that mice went to the doves' cage, because she had smelt them. Perhaps there would be a nice, lively mouse tonight. She would catch him and take him to her kittens!

Patter was running down the garden path to the cage. What a dear little mouse, with his woffly nose and long, thin tail and fine whiskers! The owl didn't see him or she would have pounced on him at once. The rat wasn't about that night or he would have had him for his dinner.

But Bubbles the cat was waiting by the cage. Patter didn't know that. He came to the cage and sniffed. He could smell CAT, but he didn't know what it was, so he wasn't afraid. He could smell bread, too, and that made his nose twitch more than ever.

Bubbles smelt him and sat there without moving even a paw. Patter ran nearer. He was just about to squeeze under the cage when he felt a strong paw pounce on him. He gave a loud squeak. "Eeeeee!"

He wriggled, but he couldn't get away. The paw held him, and he felt sharp claws sticking into him as soon as he moved. He was terribly afraid. Was this CAT?

The paw moved and scraped him away from the cage. Then hot breath came over him and something sniffed him all over. Then, oh tails and whiskers, the mouth opened and Patter went inside! He was in the cat's mouth, surrounded by sharp teeth.

He squeaked again. He was not hurt, because Bubbles hadn't scratched or bitten him. No – she wanted to take

him, whole and unhurt, to her three kittens to play with. They could chase him, pounce on him, throw him into the air, and then eat him for their supper. She would teach them what Mouse was.

She padded to the kitchen window, still holding Patter in her hot mouth. His tail hung out from between her teeth. He squeaked and squeaked. Bubbles leapt up to the window-sill and dropped down into the kitchen. She purred, and her three kittens ran to her.

She dropped Patter on the floor, and he stared round at the wondering kittens. "There," said Bubbles. "That is a mouse. Sniff him well. All mice smell the same. Then chase him and see if you can catch him."

Patter's Adventure

The kittens stared doubtfully at the mouse. Then one put out a paw to him. Patter leapt away and ran into a corner. The kitten ran after him.

Somebody was sitting in the kitchen rocking-chair. It was being rocked to and fro, to and fro. Suddenly the rocking stopped, and a voice called out in horror: "My goodness! There's a mouse running round the kitchen! My goodness!"

Up got the person in the rocking-chair and rushed out of the kitchen. She went to find Mary.

"Can you come, quickly?" she panted. "You keep pet mice, don't you, so you're not afraid of them. There's a mouse in the kitchen! Bubbles brought it in for her kittens, but it's alive and running round. I can't bear it!"

Mary went into the kitchen. She put Bubbles outside and shut the door. The kittens were still staring at the mouse, not feeling very sure about it. Patter was not at all sure about the kittens either. He felt that he would like to play with them – but they were so big!

Patter's Adventure

Mary saw him. "Oh, what a darling little field-mouse!" she said. "Go away, kittens, don't hurt it." She bent down to get it, but Patter, seeing such an enormous person suddenly bending over him, darted under a small table. Mary moved the table and put out her hand to catch Patter. He jumped away and ran right into the three kittens. Ginger put out a paw and tried to claw him. He didn't like that. He ran back under the table again.

And there Mary caught him gently in her hand. She closed her fingers round him so that only his little, woffly nose showed, and his tail hung out at the back.

"You're sweet!" she said. "I'll show you to Mummy. You're too little to be out in

the night by yourself. Whatever shall I do with you?"

She took the mouse to her mother. "Look," she said, "a baby field-mouse. Isn't he sweet? What shall I do with him? He'll be caught by Bubbles again, or an owl, if I set him free in the darkness outside."

"Well, dear, put him with your own pet mice," said her mother. "One of them died today, didn't he? Well, let this little thing take his place. He'll be quite happy with the others and much safer than running about by himself."

"Will he really?" said Mary. "I never thought of that! I'll put him into my mouse-cage now."

The mouse-cage was outside on the verandah. It was too smelly to be in the house. There were three mice there, a black, a brown, and a black-and-white. The little all-white one, Pippa, had died that morning. In the cage was a ladder for the mice to climb up and down, a dish of water and plenty of food. At the top of the cage was a shut-in place, full

of straw, which was the bedroom of the mice, very warm and cosy.

Mary lifted off the glass top, and slipped Patter inside. He was frightened now. He didn't like his adventure any more. He wanted to get back home to his mother and her nest. But he knew he would never, never find the way. Mary shone a torch into the cage and watched him.

He ran up the ladder and down. What an exciting place he had come to. But he couldn't get out of it. He sniffed here and he sniffed there – but there was no way out at all.

He could smell other mice. Where were they? He ran up a twig that was set there to lead to the bedroom and saw a round hole with straw sticking out. In a flash he was in the hole.

A ball of mice was curled up in a

corner. Patter nosed his way to it and it dissolved into three surprised little pet mice. They all sniffed at Patter.

"He's just a baby," said Frisky.

"Better make room for him," said Whisky.

"Come along then," said Nipper, and into the ball of mice crept Patter, happy and pleased. He cuddled in, wrapped his tail round everybody, stuck his nose into his paws and went to sleep.

His mother was upset when he didn't come back. "The cat's got him," she said.

Bubbles felt sure her three kittens had eaten him. "Did he taste nice?" she asked.

The three kittens felt certain that the mouse had escaped down a hole somewhere, but they didn't dare to tell their mother that. They knew they should have caught him – but they had been just a tiny bit afraid of the jumpity mouse. So they said nothing at all, but Ginger went and sat by a hole in the wall for a very long time.

Patter is still living with Frisky, Whisky and Nipper, and is as happy as the day is long. His nose is still woffly, his tail is longer than ever, and his whiskers are finer. Would you like to see him? He is a real live mouse and this is a real true story. He lives in a mouse-cage on my verandah, and we feed him every day.

"Eee!" he says and runs up his little wooden ladder to greet us. "Eeee!" Wouldn't you love a pet mouse like that?

It Really Served
Him Right

"I wish," said the orange cat loudly, "I do wish that that rag doll would go to some other toy cupboard to live."

The orange cat was a toy cat. She wasn't much bigger than a small kitten, but she was as grown-up as a cat in her ways.

The rag doll glared at the toy cat. "And *I* wish," he said, "that that silly orange cat with blue eyes would go and jump out of the window. *Blue* eyes! Whoever heard of blue eyes for a cat? Cats have green ones."

"Now, now," said the teddy-bear. "Don't start squabbling again, you two. You really ought to behave better, Raggy, because you are much older than the toy cat."

The rag doll scowled. He was a good-looking fellow for a rag doll, with a pink and white face and a shock of orange hair. He was dressed very well, too, in blue velvet trousers and a red coat. On his coat were three glass buttons, as green as grass. The rag doll was very proud of them.

"Look!" he said to the cat, pointing to his gleaming glass buttons. "Why haven't you got eyes as green as my buttons? Fancy having *blue* eyes!"

"Be quiet, Raggy. She can't help it," said the big doll. "I've got blue eyes, too."

"It's nice in a doll," said the rag doll.

"And look at that cat's tail, too – all the hairs have come off at the end!"

"Well, she couldn't help the puppy chewing her tail," said the bear. "Don't be so spiteful and bad-tempered, Raggy."

That was the worst of Raggy. He *was* so spiteful. If anyone did anything he didn't like he said spiteful things, and did them, too, if he could. When the bear grumbled at him one day, he hid behind the curtain with a big pin. And as soon as the bear came along, Raggy pinned him to the curtain so that he couldn't get away. That was the sort of thing he did.

So nobody liked him much, and they all thought him vain and silly. The orange cat disliked him very much. If she could, she always turned her back on him, and he didn't like that.

"Stuck-up creature!" he grumbled. "With her silly blue ribbon and great, staring blue eyes."

One day the toy cat found a piece of chocolate dropped on the floor. She was very pleased. She bit it into many small pieces and gave a bit to all her friends. But she didn't give even a lick to the rag doll.

"Mean thing!" he said, when he saw everyone munching chocolate. "All right, you just wait. I'll pay you back some day, yes, I will!"

Now the next week the orange cat felt worried. She couldn't see properly out of one of her blue eyes. She told the bear about it and he had a look at the eye.

"Goodness! It's coming loose!" he said. "I hope Mary notices it, cat, or it may drop off and be lost. You'd be funny with only one eye."

Mary was the little girl in whose nursery they all lived. The toy cat kept staring at her, hoping she would notice her loose eye. But she didn't.

She had just got a new book. It was called *The Adventurous Four*, and Mary couldn't stop reading it. You know how it is when you have an exciting book. You just want to go on and on reading.

So the toy cat's eye got looser and looser. At last it was hanging by only one thread, and still Mary hadn't noticed it. She was nearly at the end of her book, though, and the cat hoped

maybe her eye would hold on till Mary had finished reading. Then she would be sure to notice her toy cat's eye.

But that night, after Mary had gone to bed, the cat's eye dropped right off! She had been sitting quite still, afraid she might jerk it off – and then she had forgotten to keep still and had run across the room to speak to the bear.

She felt her eye falling out. It fell on the floor with a little thud – and then it rolled away under the couch. The cat gave a cry.

"Oh, my eye's gone! It's under the couch. Quick, get it, somebody!"

The toys all lay down and peeped under the couch. All except the rag doll. *He* wasn't going to bother himself! But suddenly he saw, quite near his right foot, something that shone blue. He stared at it. Gracious, it was the toy cat's eye! It must have rolled under the couch, out the other side, and all the way over to where the rag doll sat looking at a picture book.

He looked at the other toys. They were all lying on the floor, poking about under the couch. The toy cat was watching, crying tears out of her one eye.

Quick as lightning the rag doll put his foot over the blue glass eye. He kicked it into a corner. Then he got up, went to the corner, and, without anybody noticing, put the eye into his pocket. He was pleased.

"Now I've got the cat's eye! Good! She won't get it again, that's certain. I'll pay her back for all the things she said to me!"

He went over to the toys and pretended to look for the eye with them. But all the time he could feel it in his pocket. He wanted to laugh.

"Perhaps I'd better hide it safely somewhere," he thought suddenly. "If any of the toys found out that I had the eye I should get into dreadful trouble. They might turn me out of the nursery. Now where can I put it?"

Well, you will never guess where he hid it! It really was a very clever place. He went into the dolls' house. There was nobody there, for all the dolls were helping the cat to look for her dropped eye.

He went into the kitchen. He lifted up the lid of the tiny kettle set on the toy stove – and he dropped the eye in there. It went in nicely. Then he put the lid on it and ran out quietly. Nobody would ever, ever find the eye now, because the dolls' house dolls never used that

kettle. They had a smaller one they liked better.

The toy cat was very miserable indeed. She cried bitterly. The toys tried to comfort her. Only the rag doll didn't say anything nice. He was glad.

"How mean and unkind you are, Raggy," said everyone. But he didn't care a bit.

The next day Mary finished her book and had time to look at her toys again. And of course, she noticed at once that the toy cat had only one eye. She was very upset.

"You look *dreadful!*" she said. "You must have dropped it. I'll look around for it." But she couldn't find it, of course, because it was in the kettle.

"Now whatever shall I do with you?" said Mary to the miserable toy cat.

"You can't go about with one eye that's certain. And I haven't a blue button that would do for you. What *can* I do?"

She looked at the other toys, and she suddenly saw the rag doll, dressed so smartly in his velvet coat and trousers, with the three gleaming green buttons on his coat.

"Oh! Of *course*. I know what to do," cried Mary; and she picked up the surprised rag doll. "You can have *two* new eyes, toy cat – proper green ones, this time! I'll take off your blue one, and put on two of these beautiful green ones. You will look simply lovely!"

Well, what do you think of that? Snip, snip, went Mary's scissors; and, to the

rag doll's horror, the two top buttons of his coat fell off.

Then Mary took off the blue eye of the toy cat and put on the two green ones instead. You can't imagine how handsome the cat looked with two gleaming green eyes instead of blue ones. She stared round at the toys in delight.

"It's a pity the end of your tail is chewed, toy cat," said Mary. "It rather spoils your beauty. Oh, *I* know how I can put that right, too. Raggy, I shall snip a bit off your thick mop of hair and stick it on the end of the cat's tail."

And she did. It looked very fine there, but the rag doll felt cross and unhappy. He had lost his beautiful green buttons and a big bit of his fine mop of hair. And that awful toy cat had got them instead. She was looking at him with his own buttons for eyes. The rag doll could hardly stop himself from crying with rage.

Now the toys might have been sorry for the rag doll and tried to comfort him, if something else hadn't happened just then. Mary suddenly decided to give a party for the toy cat to celebrate her beautiful new eyes. And she took the kettle off the toy stove to fill with water so that she might boil it for tea.

And inside she found the blue eye of the toy cat. She picked it out and looked at it in astonishment, and so did all the toys.

"*Who* put that there?" said Mary. Nobody said anything. But something strange happened to the rag doll's face. It turned a deep purple. Everyone stared at him in surprise, and then they knew who had hidden the blue eye.

"So *you* hid it," said Mary. "You naughty, spiteful toy. I suppose you think I'm going to take off the toy cat's green eyes and give them back to you as buttons now that we have two blue eyes for her again. But I'm not. She can keep her green eyes now. She looks very handsome with them. As for you, it was a *very good punishment* to lose your lovely buttons and some of your hair.

And, what is more, you shan't come to the party."

"Oh, let him come," said the toy cat, so happy now because she had such beautiful green eyes that she simply couldn't be unkind to anyone. "Let him come. I'll forgive him. Give him a chance to be nice."

So he came. But he was very quiet, and sad, and well-behaved. The toys all think he may be better now. But he does feel funny when he sees the toy cat staring at him through the buttons he once wore on his own velvet coat.

The Surprising Buns

Every Saturday Mother Bustle baked some big, curranty buns for her brother, Policeman Plod-Along. He came to tea with her each Saturday afternoon, and curranty buns were his favourite tea-time dish.

He liked them freshly baked, so Mother Bustle used to bake them just before he came, and she put them out on her kitchen window-sill to cool whilst she went upstairs to put on a pretty dress.

Somebody else liked Mother Bustle's curranty buns, too. That was little Grumple Goblin, who lived in the cottage next door. He always knew when Mother Bustle was baking buns because they smelt so good. Then he would look out of his window and watch to see if the old dame put them out to cool. How delicious they looked!

Mother Bustle made them sugary on top, and she put plenty of currants inside. Grumple had tasted them once or twice, and he wished he could taste them again.

Then he discovered that Mother Bustle always went upstairs to change her dress after she had put out the buns to cool on the window-sill; and as her bedroom was at the front of the cottage and the kitchen was at the back, what could be easier than to take one or two buns off the sill when Mother Bustle was upstairs!

It was very easy. Each Saturday Grumple managed to take one or two buns off the sill. At first Mother Bustle didn't notice that any were gone. But when Grumple took four one Saturday she frowned.

"Now surely I made more buns than this!" she said and counted them. "Yes – there are four gone! Oh dear, oh dear, surely nobody is so mean as to steal a few of my curranty buns from me!"

Well, the next Saturday four more buns went and Mother Bustle couldn't imagine who could be stealing them. She was sure it wasn't Mr Hoo-Ha, who lived on her right. And it couldn't be the Grumple Goblin, surely, because he was always so polite and well-mannered. He always lifted his hat to her, shook hands politely, and asked how she was. No, no – it couldn't be the Grumple Goblin!

Well, then, who could it be? It must be some bad imp who had seen her buns on the sill and came each Saturday to take them. Mother Bustle wondered what to do about it.

Then she smiled a little to herself. "I know," she said, "I'll make my buns as usual – but I'll put some magic glue on the top of them instead of that sugary stickiness! What a shock for the thief!"

So the next Saturday she baked a batch of buns and on some of them she spread some strong magic glue. She put these to cool out on the window-

sill. The others she put to cool in the larder. Then she went upstairs as usual to change her dress.

Grumple saw the buns on the sill. Not so many as usual! He wouldn't dare to take more than two. He crept along quietly, keeping behind the bushes. He put his hands up to take two of the buns. Ah – that felt a big one – and that one, too!

Off he went to his cottage with them, and put them down on a plate. But wait – he couldn't put them down! They stuck to his hands! He couldn't get them off.

"Gracious goodness, what's happened!" said Grumple in alarm. "That silly old woman has put too much sugar on them! They're as sticky as glue!" It was no use. He couldn't get the buns off his hands. In the end he had to go out and ask Billy the goat to eat the buns away from his hands. Billy was quite pleased to do this. But even when the buns had gone the sticky stuff was still there.

Grumple couldn't pick up anything

without it sticking to him. He was really in despair. He looked at his sticky hands and suddenly felt sure that there was some kind of magic in the stickiness. He must get rid of it at once. He couldn't go on, day after day, with hands as sticky as this!

He thought he would go and see his sister, the Artful Goblin. She would be sure to know a spell to take the stickiness away. She would probably want him to do something difficult for her in return, but Grumple couldn't help that; and, anyway, he could always break his promise – a little thing like that wouldn't bother Grumple. So off he went to his sister's.

And who should be coming along to go to tea with Mother Bustle but Policeman Plod-Along, thinking joyfully of strong tea and curranty buns! He saw the Grumple Goblin and smiled at him. Mother Bustle had often told him of the polite, well-mannered goblin. He held out his hand to Grumple.

"Good afternoon!" he said. "I'm so pleased to see you. How do you do!"

Grumple shook hands without thinking – and then to his horror he found that he couldn't pull away his hand! The stickiness on it made it stick fast to Policeman Plod-Along's hand!

"Hey! What's this! Hey, leave go! Don't be silly, Grumple."

"I'm not silly. I just can't help it," said Grumple, pulling hard. "Oh, it hurts! I'm stuck to you and you're stuck to me!"

"Well, you'll have to come along to Mother Bustle's to see if she can unstick us," said Plod-Along, and he and Grumple walked hand in hand to Mother Bustle's. Grumple didn't want to go in at all, but he had to. Where Plod-Along went he had to go, too!

Mother Bustle was surprised to see the two coming hand in hand. "Well, well — are you such close friends?" she cried. "How do you do, Grumple?"

But Grumple couldn't let go Plod-Along's hand to shake hands with Mother Bustle! Plod-Along explained to his sister.

"You see, there's some sticky magic on his hand," he said. "Can't make it out! Can you do anything about it?"

Mother Bustle's sharp eyes went to Grumple's red face. "Oho! OHO!" she cried. "I think I know where that sticky magic came from. Yes, I think I know. For shame, Grumple! Did you take my buns?"

"Buns? What buns?" said Grumple, pretending he knew nothing.

"Oh, well – if you didn't take them it can't be my sticky-magic," said Mother Bustle. "I shan't be able to take it away then."

Grumple looked in desperation at Mother Bustle's grim face. He couldn't be fastened like this to Plod-Along all his life! No, he really couldn't!

"Well – I did take your buns," he said. "But I'll pay for them. So just you set me free, you horrid old woman! Then I can get my purse out!"

"WHAT'S THIS?" roared Plod-Along suddenly. "You've been taking my sister's buns? Stealing them! So you're a thief, are you? Come along to the police-station with me at once!"

Well, Grumple had to go, of course, because he couldn't take his hand away from Plod-Along's! Mother Bustle went with them, and as soon as Grumple was

safely in prison she poured some magic water over his hands and away went the stickiness at once! His hand fell away from the policeman's, and Plod-Along went outside the door and locked him in.

"Let him spend a night there," said Mother Bustle. "Just to teach him a lesson, the wicked little creature! So polite and well-mannered – and so bad-hearted underneath. I'm sure it is he who has been taking Dame Click's eggs and Mother Lucy's washing off her line!"

Grumple spent a lonely night locked up. In the morning he was allowed to go home, looking scared and miserable. When he got there Mother Bustle popped her head over the wall.

"Well, Grumple, let this be a lesson to you! And remember this – if ever I think you're taking things that don't belong to you again you'll find your hands as sticky as you did yesterday! So just you be careful!"

Mother Bustle still puts her curranty buns out on her window-sill to cool every Saturday – but since that time she hasn't missed a single bun. Grumple doesn't dare to go near them!

The Naughty Little Blacksmith

There was once a lovely village on the borders of Heyho Land called Comfy. The village of Comfy was exactly like its name. All the houses were snug and comfortable, the gardens were fine and everything grew well, and the people were friendly and happy.

So you can guess that plenty of people wanted to go and live in Comfy! But no one was allowed to unless they had work of some sort that they could do.

When Gobo wanted to live there the chief of the village said to him, "What work can you do?"

"I can bake pies and cakes and tarts," said Gobo. "I've brought one of my pies with me. Try it."

So the chief tried it and found it very good. "You can come and live here," he told Gobo. "Work hard and make cakes, pies, and tarts for us, and you will be very happy."

Another time a rich gnome called Smug wanted to buy one of the snug little houses. When the chief of Comfy asked him what work he could do, he answered in a very high and mighty voice:

"Work! I don't need to work! I've plenty of money without working."

"Well, go and spend it somewhere else," said the chief. "People are only really happy when they have work to do, and we want nobody here who cannot work."

So the rich gnome had to go away, disappointed and angry. The chief of the village watched him and laughed.

"He is lazy and fat!" thought the chief. "A little work would do him good and make him happy. Well, well – we don't want people like Smug here, that's certain!"

Now one day a small pixie called

Tiggle came to ask if he might live in the village. The chief came to see him and to ask him questions. Tiggle was very well dressed, and looked cheeky and vain.

"What work can you do?" asked the chief.

"Oh, anything!" answered Tiggle.

"What do you mean by 'anything'?" asked the chief.

"Well – just anything!" said Tiggle cheekily.

"We want a smith – can you shoe horses?" asked the chief, looking at Tiggle's soft white hands and thinking that they didn't look as if the pixie had ever done any work at all.

"Oh yes, I can shoo anything!" said

Tiggle. "I can shoo horses and donkeys and geese and flies – I'm very clever, I am!"

"Well, you can come and live in our village then," said the chief. "But mind you work hard!"

So Tiggle moved into a dear little house, well built and comfortable. He hung blue curtains at the window, put soft carpets on the floor, and a most comfortable armchair for himself by the parlour fire. Everyone came to give him a hand, for the folk of Comfy Village were the kindest in all Heyho land.

Tiggle soon settled down and was very happy. He had plenty of money to spend, he kept a little servant, and he made a great many friends.

The Naughty Little Blacksmith

Whenever the chief of the village was anywhere near, Tiggle would sigh and say, "I've worked so hard this week! I've shooed three geese, four ducks, five hens, and ever so many flies."

So people thought he had made shoes of all kinds and said he must be a very clever fellow. But the chief of the village still kept looking at Tiggle's soft white hands, and wondered how anyone could have hands like that if he really did such a lot of hard work.

"I'd like to see the shoes you make, Tiggle," said the chief one day. "I'll come along and see some tomorrow. I've a duck with a lame foot – perhaps one of your shoes would do for it."

Well, that gave Tiggle a great shock,

for, as you may guess, he had never made a shoe for anything in his life.

He said goodbye very quickly, and caught the next bus to the town over the hill. There he spent a good deal of money on red, yellow, and blue shoes of all kinds. He put them into his bag and went home. He arranged all the shoes in his parlour, and the next day, when the chief of Comfy came knocking at the door, he found Tiggle busy sewing a button on a shoe.

"Dear me!" said the chief, looking all round. "What a lot of shoes! I like this little blue pair!"

He picked up the blue shoes, turned them upside down, and looked at them. On the sole was stamped the name of

the shop where Tiggle had bought the shoes! The chief put down the shoes and looked at Tiggle, who was still busy with the button.

"So you made all these shoes, Tiggle?" he said.

"Yes, sir," said Tiggle, most untruthfully. He went very red, and hung his head over the shoe he was holding.

"Really?" said the chief, and walked to the door. "Well, tomorrow I'll bring a few things for you to shoe, Tiggle. And I shall be sorry for you if you can't do the job!"

The next morning Tiggle got such a shock – for up the hill to his house came a great crowd of people.

The chief came first, leading his lame duck. Then came others, some with a horse, some with a dog or cat, some with hens and geese!

The chief knocked on Tiggle's door. "Come out, Tiggle!" he cried. "We want to see you do some work. We've brought a few creatures for you to shoe!"

Tiggle opened the door and looked at all the animals. "I can't work today," he said. "I don't feel well."

Everybody crowded into Tiggle's little garden. Somebody's goat began to eat the flowers, and the hens scratched up a bed of lettuce.

Tiggle saw them and was very angry. "Take your horrid creatures away!" he shouted.

"Not till you've shod them all," said the chief. "You said you could shoe anything, Tiggle. Was that true?"

"Yes, quite true," said Tiggle sulkily. "But I didn't mean what *you* meant, that's all. I *can* shoo anything!"

"You're not telling the truth," said everybody. The goat ate all Tiggle's sweet-peas and began on the tomato plants. Tiggle was dreadfully upset, and very angry indeed.

"I *am* telling the truth!" he shouted. "I'll show you! *I'll* show you! Watch me shooing the goat, to start with!"

Tiggle rushed at the alarmed goat, waved his hands at him, and yelled loudly. "Shoo, goat! Shoo, shoo, SHOO! Shoo, goat!"

The goat shooed in fright. He jumped right over the wall and ran down the street. Everyone stared with wide-open eyes and mouth. Tiggle shouted at them.

"Well, didn't I shoo the goat? Didn't I? Now I'll shoo all the other creatures you brought to be shooed! Shoo, duck! Shoo, hen! Shoo, shoo, shoo, geese! Ah, you bad creatures, you've eaten my carrots. Shoo, I tell you, shoo! And shoo, you dogs and cats; and shoo, you silly horse, eating my grass. SHOO!"

All the animals and birds fled away

in fright. They jumped over the wall, squeezed under the gate, flew over the hedge – anything to get away from the shouting pixie.

"Now stop this, you bad pixie," said the chief, very sternly. "You deceived us. You didn't deserve to live in our happy little village. You . . ."

"I won't be talked to like this!" shouted Tiggle, who was in a fine old temper now. "Shoo, all of you! shoo! SHOO! I said I could shoo anything, and so I can. I'll shoo the lot of you! Shoo! SHOO!"

"Ho, ho! So that's how you are going to behave, is it?" cried the chief, losing his temper too. "Well, we can do a bit of shooing, too!"

He slipped off his shoe. Everyone else

took off a shoe too, and grinned. They knew what was coming.

"Shoo, Tiggle, shoo! Shoe! Shoe!" cried the chief, and he lifted his leather shoe and gave Tiggle such a smack with it that he jumped high in the air and howled with pain. "How do you like our way of shooing, Tiggle? Shoo! Shoo!"

Everyone tried to get in a smack at bad little Tiggle, and cried, "Shoo! Shoo! Here's a shoe for you! Smack, smack! Shoo, shoo!"

Tiggle ran down the path to the gate. Smack, smack, shoo, shoo! The goat peeped over the wall and laughed. The geese cackled loudly. Tiggle yelled and shouted, and ran as fast as he could out of the gate.

"It doesn't pay to be deceitful!" cried the people after him. "You'd better be honest next time, Tiggle! Shoo, shoo, shoo!"

Tiggle caught the next bus, crying big tears down his nose. "I was silly," he sobbed. "I daren't go back. I've lost all my goods and left my money behind. Now I shall really have to go to work."

Well, it didn't do him any harm. He went to help a blacksmith, so he really *is* shoeing something now. Maybe one day he'll go back to the village of Comfy and start all over again, honest and hard working. But I think I know what everyone will shout if they see him again. Do you?

Yes – shoo, shoo, shoo!

Little Mr Tuppeny

Little Mr Tuppeny walked down the road stooping as he always did. He looked very gloomy.

"What I want is a bit of luck," said Tuppeny. "Some people have plenty. I never seem to have any."

He plodded on down the road on his way home. "There's my wife ill again. There's the boy without good shoes to wear, he's grown out of his old ones. There's Ellie wanting to go to the school party and hasn't got a nice dress to wear."

On and on he went, thinking his gloomy thoughts. "I'm a first-rate gardener and all I've got for a job is just two days' work a week at that mean

167

Miss White's. Think of that – two days a week!"

He turned the corner and almost bumped into a bicycle. He stepped hurriedly to one side and lost his balance. Down he went.

He sat heavily in a puddle and got up quickly. "There now – I have to meet a bicycle tearing round the corner, and I have to fall, and I have to go into a puddle and soak my trousers. And they're the only pair I've got! I never have any luck, never."

He walked on, his eyes on the ground because he stooped so much. And then he saw something that made him stop and stare.

Lying by the roadside, half-hidden by grass, was a pearl necklace! It glimmered up at Tuppeny, and he stared with wide eyes.

"A pearl necklace!" he whispered and picked it up. "My, that's worth a lot of money. A whole lot. Why, if I sold this it would keep my family all the year. I could look for a very fine job and wait

until the right one came along. I could take Mrs Tuppeny to the sea and get her well again."

He looked at the necklace in his hand. "You are valuable enough to buy shoes for Joe and a new dress for Ellie," he said. "You must be worth a hundred pounds at least! Think of that! Oh, what couldn't I do with a hundred pounds."

He slipped the necklace into his pocket and walked on, thinking hard. He made all kinds of plans. He would buy himself a new suit so that he might look tidier when he went after good jobs. He would buy some paint and paint his cottage – and get that chimney mended and the hole in the roof done.

And then, just as he got to the end of the lane and saw his cottage nearby, he stopped. He had been trying not to think a thought that was at the back of his mind, trying very hard indeed. But now the thought had come right to the front and he had to think it.

"This necklace doesn't belong to *me*. It belongs to somebody else. I ought to take it back. I've no right to sell it and take the money. I'd be as bad as a thief."

Tuppeny groaned. "There now – all my plans gone! No new suit, no holiday by the sea, no new shoes or new dress! I must send the necklace to the police station, that's what I must do. Oh, what a pity I'm an honest man! If only I were dishonest – think of the things I could do for my wife and children – and myself, too!"

But it wasn't any good. Tuppeny was honest and he always had been. He couldn't turn into a thief all at once like that. Why, whatever would his gentle little wife say!

Poor Tuppeny. He walked into the kitchen looking so gloomy that his wife was quite startled.

"Tuppeny! What's the matter? Have you lost your job at Miss White's?"

"No," said Tuppeny. "Worse than that, wife, I've had the chance of giving you a holiday by the sea, and buying the boy shoes, and Ellie a dress – and getting myself a new suit and a new job – and mending the roof and buying new paint for the house – and I've thrown the chance away! Ah, I'm a poor husband for you."

"What do you mean, Tuppeny?" asked

his wife. He told her. "See this pearl necklace? I found it. It must be worth a hundred pounds. If I kept it and sold it I'd get all the things we want. But I'm going to send it to the police station. See? I'm throwing away the chance of giving my family some of the things they badly want. I tell you, I'm a poor husband, wife."

"I love you because you're a dear, honest, good man," said Mrs Tuppeny and she hugged him. "I couldn't love a thief."

"And dear me, *I* couldn't love *you* if you wanted me to keep the necklace and sell it!" said Mr Tuppeny looking suddenly cheerful. "Where's Joe? Hey, Joe, take this along to the police station and hand it in. Tell them I found it in the lane."

"Will there be a reward, Dad?" asked Joe. Tuppeny smiled. He hadn't thought of a reward. Yes, there might be. Ah – that would be a bit of a help.

"Maybe there is," he said. "If so, new shoes for you, Joe, and a new dress for

Ellie! You go along now and give in the necklace."

Joe ran off with the necklace. He came to the police station. He knew the policeman there because he was the father of one of his school friends.

"Mr Peters, sir," he said. "My father found this necklace today, and told me to bring it here. Is there a reward offered for the finder?"

Mr Peters took the necklace. He laughed. "Why, this isn't worth more than a pound," he said. "It must be Sarah Joyce's. Her mother came in to see if anyone had brought it in, because the child is so fond of it. There won't be any reward, I'm afraid."

Joe went home sadly. "It's not worth more than a pound, Dad," he said. "There's no reward."

"There now – honest for nothing!" said Tuppeny. "Not even a reward. I'm an unlucky fellow – no good to anyone!"

Ah, but wait! The next day there came a knock at the Tuppenys' door. Mrs Tuppeny opened it. Outside stood Mr Joyce, the father of the little girl who had lost her necklace. He smiled at Mrs Tuppeny.

"Good day," he said. "I came to thank your husband for returning Sarah's necklace, and to ask if he's got a job, because my gardener has gone. I dismissed him for dishonesty – everyone

knows that. And this time I want an honest fellow, so . . ."

"Oh, sir! But Mr Tuppeny wouldn't be a good enough gardener for your lovely place!" cried little Mrs Tuppeny. "If you'd just take him on two or three days a week, sir, that would be wonderful."

"No," said Mr Joyce. "I want a full-time gardener, and I'd rather have a willing, honest fellow who doesn't know everything, than someone who thinks he knows a lot and can't even be trusted not to take lettuces and peas home each night to sell! You tell your husband to come and see me."

Well, Tuppeny went. Mr Joyce liked Tuppeny, and Tuppeny liked Mr Joyce. They were both kind, honest and friendly people, and Tuppeny went home very happy indeed.

"I've got a fine job, dear," he said, "and my first week's wages in advance. Here you are – shoes for Joe, a dress for Ellie, and see you buy something for yourself, too. My, I'm the luckiest man in the world!"

"And to think that a pound necklace did all that!" said Mrs Tuppeny. "But no – that's wrong, Tuppeny – it wasn't the necklace that did it – it was your own honesty in taking it back when you thought it was worth a hundred pounds. You've turned our luck, Tuppeny, you have, you have!"

She was right. Their luck turned from that very day. You just never know, do you, what will happen when you choose to do the right thing, like little Mr Tuppeny.

Take Firm Hold of the Nettle

Ronnie was in disgrace. He had forgotten to take the right book home for his homework, so at school in the morning he hadn't known his lesson.

Mr Brown, the master, had been angry with him. "You've got good brains! You must be lazy if you don't know your lesson today! Stay in after school and learn it."

So Ronnie had had to stay in after school and that had made him late home for dinner. His mother had wanted to know why, of course, and he had been afraid to tell her that he had been kept in.

"Oh – I didn't know the time," he said.

"Ronnie, you've got a watch that

keeps good time!" scolded his mother. "I told you it was a nice, hot dinner to-day and I told you I wanted to catch the two o'clock bus. Now your dinner is spoilt, and I shan't be able to catch the bus. You're selfish and unkind."

Ronnie was miserable as he ate his dinner. Mr Brown had called him lazy, and he wasn't. His mother had called him unkind and selfish, and he wasn't. People were always accusing him of being things he wasn't.

He thought of the week before. Three of the boys had been going home together, and Ronnie was one of them. Tom had found a parcel in the road, dropped by the postman, and he had actually opened it!

Ronnie hadn't liked to say anything. In the parcel were bars of chocolate! Tom had divided them up and given each of the other two boys the same as himself. Ronnie knew it was dishonest, but he didn't like to say no.

"They might laugh at me!" he thought, "and I do hate being laughed at. I know what I'll do. I'll take these bars home, but I won't eat them. Then I shan't be sharing in Tom's dishonesty."

So he had taken the bars home and hidden them – but, alas, his mother had found them, and soon she had discovered about Tom's find and how he had opened the parcel. She wouldn't believe that Ronnie didn't mean to be dishonest and had just taken them home and not meant to eat them. She went to Tom's mother and told her, and Tom, Ronnie and the other boy had all had a terrible scolding.

"And when we went and owned up to the postman, as Mother made us, he called us all dishonest," thought Ronnie. "And I wasn't. I didn't want to take the chocolate and I never ate one bit. Why do people keep thinking I am what I'm not?"

He went off to school, still miserable. He hadn't washed his hands, and Mr Brown saw them as soon as he took his place in class.

"Ronnie! Your hands are too dirty to bear looking at! Go and wash them!"

Ronnie went to wash them. He ran the hot water and took up the soap. He squeezed it in his hands – and to his horror it flew straight out of the cloakroom window and disappeared! He stood still and stared after it.

He didn't dare to go and get it, in case

Mr Brown saw him. He thought he'd better say nothing at all. So he washed his hands as best he could, wiped most of the dirt off on the towel and went back to class. Then another boy was sent to wash his hands, too, and he came back at once to say there was no soap there!

"Of course – that would happen!" thought Ronnie in despair. Mr Brown turned to him. "What did you do with the soap, Ronnie?" he said.

"There – there wasn't any there," said Ronnie.

"Then why didn't you come and tell me that?" demanded Mr Brown. "You are a very stupid boy. I don't expect you to be able to wash your hands if there is

no soap. What a silly, stupid boy you're turning out to be, Ronnie!"

Ronnie went very red. He wasn't silly, he wasn't stupid. He knew that. Oh dear, people always kept saying he was what he wasn't! He would never, never be able to stop them. It was just his bad luck.

He went out into the fields that afternoon after school. He wanted to be by himself. Things seemed to go wrong all the time. Perhaps he was one of the unlucky people of the world!

He sat down and heaved such an enormous sigh that somebody heard it. It was the gardener on the other side of the hedge. He had been sitting in the

garden there, smoking his pipe, when he heard Ronnie's enormous sigh.

He peered through the hedge and saw a very miserable boy. "Hey, there!" called the old fellow. "What's up with *you?* You look like I do when the frost's got all my nice little tomato plants! You come along in here and tell me what's up with you. Your face is enough to turn the milk sour."

Ronnie squeezed through the hedge. "Well, I should like to tell *somebody*," he said. "You see, it's like this – everybody thinks I'm selfish, or lazy, or stupid, or unkind, or dishonest, or something – all things I'm not! It's just a lot of mistakes. But I don't know how to make people think differently. I'm afraid I'm born to have bad luck!"

"Rubbish! Nonsense! Fiddlesticks!" said the old gardener, puffing away at his pipe. "Nobody's born to have bad luck. Now, you tell me your troubles and I'll show you how to mend them!"

So Ronnie told the old fellow all about forgetting his homework book, and being kept in, and getting home late and preventing his mother from catching the bus, and all about the soap that flew out of his hands, and how Mr Brown called him stupid, and he even told him about the parcel Tom had found and opened, which had made people call Ronnie dishonest, when he really, really wasn't! The old man listened and didn't interrupt at all. When Ronnie had finished he nodded his head two or three times.

"What's wrong with *you*," he said, "is that you don't know the right way to take hold of a nettle!"

Ronnie stared in surprise. What an odd thing to say! The old man nodded at him again. "No – I'm not mad, my boy! I've seen plenty like you, afraid to take hold of a nettle the right way. Now I'll show you what I mean. See that stinging-nettle by you?"

"Yes," said Ronnie. "If I touch it it will sting me."

"Ah yes, so it will – but if you know the right way to handle a nettle it won't sting you," said the old gardener. "Now you look here – see that leaf, full of stinging barbs that will send poison down into your hand? Well, look – I've

got hold of it – see? And see, it hasn't stung me at all. Not a bit of it!"

"Why hasn't it?" asked Ronnie, surprised.

"Because I took hold of it *firmly*," said the old man. "Nettles are like all annoying, upsetting things – you have to take them firmly and they can't do you any harm. If you're afraid of them, and don't face up to them, they'll sting you good and proper and make you as miserable as can be. No, my boy, you haven't been handling your nettles properly!"

"I don't quite see what you mean," said Ronnie. "I haven't any nettles."

"Oh yes you have," said the old man. "That was a nettle, your forgetting your homework book, and you let it sting you well, time and again! You got stung by your master's sharp words and your mother's anger! Now what you should have done to that nettle was to take hold of it firmly so that it couldn't sting at all!"

"Why – how could I do that?" asked Ronnie.

"Well, when you knew you'd forgotten your book and couldn't do your lesson, you should have gone to your master the very next morning and told him – and you should have said you were sorry, but you'd learn the lesson in Break, if that would do. That nettle wouldn't have stung you then! You wouldn't have been kept in, you wouldn't have upset your mother. That was a good old stinging-nettle you touched!"

"Oh, I see what you mean!" said Ronnie. "But – how could I have tackled that other stinging-nettle – when Tom opened that parcel and gave me the chocolate?"

"Grasp that nettle firmly, too, and it

wouldn't sting you!" said the gardener. "You should have said, 'No, not for me, Tom. I'm not one for that kind of thing and, what's more, my friends don't do that kind of thing, either!' And do you know what would have happened? Why, I guess young Tom would have packed that parcel up again, all red about the face, and gone to find the postman!"

"I wish I'd done that," said Ronnie. "I was afraid."

"Yes, you touched the nettle so timidly that it stung you for days!" said the old man. "And that soap, now! Well, it's an accident that might happen to anyone, having the soap fly out of their hands! A silly little nettle, that one! What's to prevent you going to your master and saying, 'Sir, I'm sorry, but the soap flew out of my hands and jumped out of the window. May I get it?'"

"I didn't dare to say that," said Ronnie.

"A pity!" said the old man. "Mr Brown would have had a good laugh and said: 'Hurry and get it, and don't let the soap play tricks again!' I know Mr Brown, and he likes a boy that grasps a nettle well."

"I think you're very wise," said Ronnie, after a bit. "How did you get to know all this?"

"Well, a gardener soon gets to know the way to treat nettles," said the old man, getting up. "And he should know how to treat the nettles that grow in our lives, too. You take hold of them firmly, wherever they grow, my boy – and, my word, you won't find people calling you names you don't deserve any more!"

Ronnie ran home. He was late, of course, and his mother looked up crossly. "Ronnie – I suppose you were late just to annoy me again! It's too bad of you!"

"A nettle, a nettle!" thought Ronnie.

"Take hold of it firmly."

He spoke out loud. "Mother, I'll tell you exactly what happened – and if you like to scold me or punish me afterwards, well, you must, and I'll try and make up to you for being late. You see – I met an old man, and ..." Ronnie told his mother everything. She listened in surprise. When he had finished she patted him on the shoulder.

"I wish *I'd* been able to tell you all that, Ronnie," she said. "I see now I should have, because you didn't know. Yes, grasp your nettles firmly, and nothing is ever quite so bad as it seems. You can get over all kinds of disappointments and difficulties if only you tackle them firmly! I'll help you! You'll do fine, you'll see!"

Well, that was a year ago, and Ronnie certainly is doing fine! He failed in the scholarship exam, but did he mope and grumble about it? Not he! He grasped that nettle firmly and said: "I'm not going to be beaten! I'll sit for it again!"

He did, and he won it. A nasty, tough

nettle, but he knew how to take hold of it!

Then his mother fell ill and there were such big bills for pills and medicines that Ronnie had to go without the new bicycle he so badly wanted. A very annoying nettle, because his old bike had fallen to bits.

What did he do? Well, he offered to work on Farmer Straw's land for two hours after school each day, and in a few weeks' time he had enough money to buy himself a bicycle!

Ronnie treats all his nettles like that. And now nobody calls him names he doesn't deserve. Instead, Mr Brown says he is clever, hard-working and

trustworthy. His friends say he is a born leader, as honest as the day, and quite fearless in sticking up for what he thinks is right. And his mother – well, you'll have to ask her what *she* thinks, and she'll tell you a lot. It would make Ronnie blush to hear her! He is great friends with the old gardener now and very grateful to him for his good advice.

"I do wish you could tell every boy and girl how to take hold of their nettles!" he said to the old gardener. Well, the old fellow can't do that, so I said I would. And I have, haven't I? Take hold of your nettles the right way and they won't sting you at all!